"He's behind us, Lucas!" Hannah said, fear in her voice.

"We'll be okay," Lucas promised as he drove faster.

Tears sprang to her eyes as memories gripped her. She couldn't escape, not from the man in flannel who kept coming after her, not from her mother's hateful words, not from the mistakes she had made when it came to her heart.

"He's gaining." Hannah watched the car draw even closer.

The driver turned on his bright lights. The reflection flashed in Lucas's eyes, blinding him momentarily.

"There's no getting away from him." Fear ate through her gut. She clutched the console with one hand and the dashboard with the other, trying to steady herself as the car bounced even more over the pitted roadway.

"Hold on," Lucas warned as he maneuvered the car around the broken asphalt. "A small dirt road veers to the right around the next curve. We'll pull off there."

"He'll follow us, Lucas. We'll be sitting ducks."

The road ahead went dark as they rounded the bend.

Fear gripped her anew. "What happened?"

He glanced at her. "I won't let anyone hurt you. That's a promise."

Debby Giusti is an award-winning Christian author who met and married her military husband at Fort Knox, Kentucky. Together they traveled the world, raised three wonderful children and have now settled in Atlanta, Georgia, where Debby spins tales of mystery and suspense that touch the heart and soul. Visit Debby online at debbygiusti.com, blog with her at seekerville.blogspot.com and craftieladiesofromance.blogspot.com, and email her at Debby@DebbyGiusti.com.

Books by Debby Giusti

Love Inspired Suspense

Amish Protectors

Amish Refuge
Undercover Amish

Military Investigations

The Officer's Secret
The Captain's Mission
The Colonel's Daughter
The General's Secretary
The Soldier's Sister
The Agent's Secret Past
Stranded
Person of Interest
Plain Danger
Plain Truth

Visit the Author Profile page at Harlequin.com for more titles.

UNDERCOVER AMISH

DEBBY GIUSTI

DISCARD

 HARLEQUIN® LOVE INSPIRED® SUSPENSE

Recycling programs
for this product may
not exist in your area.

LOVE INSPIRED BOOKS

ISBN-13: 978-0-373-67852-5

Undercover Amish

Copyright © 2017 by Deborah W. Giusti

www.Harlequin.com

Printed in U.S.A.

Praise be to the Lord,
for He has heard my cry for mercy.
The Lord is my strength and my shield;
my heart trusts in Him, and He helps me.
My heart leaps for joy,
and with my song I praise Him.
–Psalms 28:6-7

To My Husband—My Hero

ONE

"Hey, lady, that woman on TV looks just like you."

Hannah Miller ignored the wizened old man with the scruffy beard and bloodshot eyes, who undoubtedly was talking to her since she was the only woman in the gas station. Instead of responding, she handed her credit card to the attendant behind the counter. "Twenty dollars on pump four."

Averting her gaze from not only the older man but also the cluster of guys ogling the model on the cover of the latest edition of a men's sports magazine, she squared her shoulders, raised her chin and hoped she looked more confident than she felt. A truck stop off the interstate was the last place Hannah wanted to be in the dead of night, but she needed gas. She also needed to find her sister Miriam and to learn the details of her mother's death as well as the whereabouts of her youngest sister, Sarah, who had disappeared along with Miriam.

Refusing to be deterred, the old guy with the beard pointed to the flat-screen TV hanging on the wall. "Check it out, lady."

As much as she didn't want to respond to his comment, she couldn't stop from glancing at the television. Her heart lurched and a tiny gasp escaped her lips. Her middle sister's face stared back at her from the thirty-two-inch screen.

A reporter, holding a microphone, stepped toward Miriam as the news video continued to play. "Ms. Miller, do you have any comment about the man who murdered your mother?"

"No comment." Miriam pushed past the reporter and climbed aboard a Gray Line bus.

"The suspected killer is dead," the man with the mike continued, "along with a deputy sheriff who was involved in Leah Miller's death. Now her daughter Miriam is leaving Willkommen. A spokesperson for the mayor's office said the tragedy is an isolated incident. The crime rate in the town and surrounding Amish community is low, and tourists shouldn't be discouraged from visiting the area."

The video ended and the late-night news anchor returned to the screen. "That footage, shot six weeks ago, is the last taken of Miriam Miller, although there is speculation she returned to Willkommen and is hiding out in the North Georgia mountains. The police now suspect the carjacking that claimed Leah Miller's life could be tied to the disappearance eight months earlier of Rosie Glick, an Amish girl believed at the time to have run off with her *Englisch* boyfriend."

Hannah's heart pounded and a roar filled her ears. Seeing the news feed made the information she'd learned about her family only hours earlier even more real. She desperately needed space to recover her composure, but the insistent bearded man sidled closer.

"'Spect your last name must be Miller." He raised his voice. "Except for your blue eyes, you look so much alike that you've got to be kin to that woman on the news whose mother was killed. Gunned down in a carjacking was the story I heard."

Hannah pursed her lips and hoped her icy glare would convince the attendant who still held her credit card not to divulge her name. Evidently the kid behind the counter was smart enough to pick up on her cues. He returned her card without comment.

She glanced at the group of men near the magazine rack who had stopped perusing the cover model to stare at her. Feeling totally exposed, she returned the credit card to her wallet, all the while her neck tingled and heat seared her cheeks.

One of the men, dressed in a blue flannel shirt and navy hoodie, shrugged out of the group and hurried outside. If only the other men would leave, as well. Not that they were doing anything wrong, but the last thing Hannah wanted was to call attention to herself.

She tucked her wallet into her purse, grabbed the sales receipt and hurried into the ladies' room, needing a private place to come to terms with what had happened. Her head throbbed and she fought to control the tears that burned her eyes. Her mother was dead, Miriam was gone and her younger sister Sarah had disappeared. When Hannah had left home three years ago, Sarah had just turned eighteen.

Deriding herself for her insensitivity to her family's need, Hannah hung her head in shame. Why hadn't she tried to contact them in all that time? In spite of the angry words exchanged the night she'd left and her fear that law enforcement had been called in, Hannah should have been the better person and made an attempt to reconnect. For so long she'd blamed her mother and Miriam. Now they were gone from her life and her heart ached too much to blame anyone but herself.

Hannah had been selfish and thinking of her

own needs, not the good of the family. Although the three girls raised by a flighty, self-absorbed mother hardly deserved the name "family." The disjointed reality of their dysfunctional life had, at times, seemed anything but close-knit or loving.

Plus, the old man was wrong. Any resemblance she had to Miriam was slight. After what she had learned the night she'd left home, it was no wonder she had always felt like an outsider. The accusation and the memory of the secret her mother had revealed remained an open wound.

The last thing she'd expected to find today on her cell phone was Miriam's garbled voice mail. Her sister's heartbreaking message—at least what Hannah could decipher—had been almost too much to bear.

According to the television footage, Miriam hadn't been seen in Willkommen since she'd boarded the bus six weeks ago. The possibility of finding either sister seemed remote, yet Hannah wouldn't give up her search until she found Miriam *and* Sarah.

Needing to get back on the road, Hannah splashed cold water on her face, wiped it dry with a paper towel and hurried to her car, grateful that the older, bearded guy, now chatting with the men by the magazine rack, failed to notice her departure.

Nearing her car, Hannah sensed she wasn't alone and turned to see the man in blue flannel. He glanced at her through narrowed eyes before he opened the door to his black Tahoe and settled into the driver's seat. Something about the guy chilled her blood. Was it his bushy brows and pensive stare or his long hair pulled into a ponytail? His jeans and work boots were crusted with Georgia clay, making him look like he belonged on a backhoe instead of in the well-detailed SUV.

Unnerved by the man's penetrating gaze, she unscrewed the gas cap, inserted the nozzle and began pumping, all the while watching the guy pull his black SUV onto the roadway, heading toward the highway. For whatever reason, she felt a sense of relief.

Once her tank was full, she slipped behind the wheel of her small, four-door sedan and turned left toward Willkommen. Surely the town couldn't be too far away.

The road was windy and narrow and angled up the mountain. A sign for Pine Lodge Mountain Resort caught her attention. Closed For Renovation read the small banner that hung over the larger placard.

A light drizzle began to fall. Hannah flipped on the windshield wipers and squinted into the night. If only visibility was better. The temperature dropped as the elevation increased. She upped the heater, but even with the warm air blowing straight at her, she still felt cold and totally alone.

Usually she welcomed solitude. Tonight, she found the night too dark and eerie. Had it been along this road where her mother had been killed?

Her gut tightened and another tide of hot tears burned her eyes. She blinked them back, swallowed the lump that filled her throat and focused even more intently on the narrow mountain road.

A warning light flashed on her dash. She leaned closer and tapped the glass, unsure of what was wrong. Her heart pounded as she watched the temperature gauge rise. She clicked the heater off but the needle continued to climb.

She groaned, pulled to the side of the road and killed the engine. Staring into the darkness, she gulped down a lump of fear. She was too far from the gas station to walk back, and she hadn't passed another car for more than twenty minutes. If only someone would happen along.

"Lord—" she bowed her head "—I'm just starting on my walk of faith, but I trust You're with me. Send help."

She glanced up to see headlights in the rear-view mirror.

"Thank You, Lord." She exited her car, grateful when the vehicle pulled to a stop behind her sedan. A man stepped to the pavement. Hannah squinted in the glare from his headlights and put her hand to her forehead to shield her eyes. Something about the guy stirred her memory. He neared and her pulse ricocheted as she recognized the blue flannel shirt.

His car had been headed for the highway when he'd pulled out of the gas station. Why had he turned around?

"Looks like you've got a problem." His voice was deep with a hint of Southern twang.

"You're right about a problem," she replied, keeping her tone even and hoping he didn't hear the tremble in her voice. "My engine seems to have overheated."

"Mind if I take a look under the hood?"

"Sure. Thanks." Only Hannah wasn't sure about anything, especially the strange man with the ponytail.

"You wanna pop the hood?" he asked.

She tugged on the release and then stood aside as he peered into the engine.

"Looks like you've got a hole in your radiator."

"But how—?"

"No telling, lady. Willkommen's not far. I'll give you a lift."

An overwhelming sense of dread washed over her. "If you could send someone from a service station, I'd prefer to stay with my vehicle."

"There might not be another car along for hours," he cautioned.

Wary of his advice, she held up her hand. "If you could send help, I'd be most grateful."

"I can't leave you out here." His smile seemed more like a sneer. "Come on, lady. I won't hurt you."

"I never said you would." She stepped back from the car and from the man whose lips suddenly curved into a seductive grin.

Her pulse raced. Fear threaded through her veins.

He moved closer and held out his hand. "Sure you wouldn't like a ride to town?"

"No, thanks."

"Come on, honey."

She wasn't his honey, nor did she like the tone of his voice.

Flicking her gaze over her shoulder, she eyed the thick forest that edged the roadway. Would it provide cover? Enough cover?

He stepped closer and reached for her hand.

She drew back. "What do you want?" she demanded.

"Information. That old guy at the gas station

was right. You've got to be related to the woman on the news."

Hannah shook her head. "I don't know what you're talking about."

He retrieved his cell from his pocket and pulled up a photo. "This is the woman. You look just like her."

Hannah peered at the picture of her sister and fought to control her emotions, seeing Miriam's bruised forehead and her matted hair.

The lewd man stepped closer. "She left Willkommen weeks ago. Some folks say she returned. If so, I need to find her."

"I…I can't help you."

His face darkened. "Look, lady, I'm working with the police. They need to question her."

She didn't believe him, but instead of arguing she squared her shoulders and raised her chin. "Why don't you just climb in your car and return to town?"

The finality of her tone must have convinced him she wouldn't change her mind. He started to step back but then lunged for her. "Where is she? Where's Miriam?"

Hannah screamed. He grabbed her arm. She slipped out of his hold and ran into the woods. The tall pines blocked the moonlight and darkness surrounded her like a pall.

She tripped, righted herself and ran on.

His footfalls came after her, drawing closer.

She increased her speed, not knowing where she was headed or what she would find.

Lord, save me.

A clearing lay ahead. The moon broke through the dark cloud cover, bathing the rolling landscape in light that would mark her as an easy target if she continued on. She angled away from the clearing and forged deeper into the forest. Stumbling over a branch, she threw out her hand to block her fall. Her fingers brushed against a ladder.

She felt the rungs and stared up into the night, seeing the faint outline of a platform at least twelve feet off the ground.

Movement in the brush warned of the man's approach.

Hannah scurried up the ladder and climbed onto the platform. Lying down, she placed her ear to the floorboards and worked to keep her breathing shallow. Even her labored pull of air could alert him to her whereabouts.

The guy ran straight ahead into the clearing. Before the moon passed behind the clouds, Hannah could make out his features. Why was the guy interested in Miriam?

Dear God, don't let him find me.

Her heart pounded so hard she thought it would surely shake the platform.

The man backtracked. He stopped at the foot of the ladder. The platform swayed as he stepped onto the first rung, then the second and the third.

She was trapped at twelve feet above ground and about to be found out by a man intent on doing her harm.

Be still, she chastised her heart, ricocheting in her chest.

She could hear his raspy breath as he stopped his climb and remained poised halfway up the ladder.

"Where…are…you?" he demanded, his voice low and menacing. "I know you ran this way, but I don't see you anywhere."

A lump filled her throat. In half a second he would scramble to the top, grab her and—

She gritted her teeth to keep from screaming.

Leaves rustled behind the stand as if someone or something was scurrying through the fallen debris, heading back toward the parked cars.

"I've got you now," he whispered, sounding jubilant. In a flash, he climbed down the ladder and ran to catch up to whatever squirrel or possum or raccoon that had saved Hannah, at least for the moment.

Over the roar in her ears, she could hear him disappear into the night. Opening her mouth, she gulped air and trembled from the fear that had wrapped her tightly in its hold.

Thank You, God.

She lay still for a long time, listening to the forest and allowing her anxiety to calm. Breathing in the serenity of the moment, she closed her eyes and, at some point, drifted into a light slumber.

With a jerk, she awoke. Rubbing her neck, she started to sit up. Just that quickly, the sound of footsteps returned. Her gut churned and she bit her lip to keep from moaning in distress.

After all this time, why was he coming back?

Again, she flattened her body against the platform, willed her heart to remain calm and blinked back hot tears that stung her eyes.

This time he would find her. He neared, then stepped onto the ladder, one foot, then another and another as he climbed higher.

Faintly in the distance, she could hear the rev of a car engine as a vehicle headed down the mountain, but all she could think about was the man on the ladder.

He stopped for half a second, then raised a rifle and laid it on the wooden deck.

Her chance. Her only chance. She grabbed the weapon and pointed it straight at the wide-brimmed hat and full face that appeared over the edge of the platform.

* * *

A sliver of moonlight peered from between the clouds as Lucas Grant climbed over the top of the ladder onto the deer stand. Just that fast, his heart stopped, seeing the woman staring at him wide-eyed. Her long hair and oval face made him think of Olivia.

Then he saw the rifle—his .30-30 Winchester—aimed at his gut.

"Put the gun down, lady, before one of us gets hurt."

"Who are you?" she demanded, her gaze wary and tight with fear. Although she squared her shoulders and raised her jaw, the hint of uncertainty was evident in her voice.

"Lucas Grant. This is my property. My deer stand." He let the information settle for half a second then added, "Seems you're trespassing. So, if you know what's good for you, ma'am, you best hand over my .30-30."

He pursed his lips and pulled in a breath as she hesitated longer than he would have liked.

"I won't hurt you, ma'am, and I don't aim to do you harm."

She tilted her pretty head, wrinkled her brow and looked at him through what appeared, even in the dim moonlight, to be troubled eyes.

"You're Amish?" she asked, the surprise evident in her voice.

He glanced down at the black trousers and blue shirt, knowing it was the suspenders that made her come to that conclusion, along with the wide-brimmed felt hat and the black outer coat that hung open.

"I work at an Amish bed-and-breakfast," he said, unwilling to provide more information.

Her brow wrinkled even more. "So you're not Amish."

He shrugged. "Call me Amish in training."

"What?"

He held out his hand. "Ma'am, let's get rid of the weapon and then we can make our introductions."

Instead of reassuring the woman, his comment seemed to have the opposite effect. She gripped the barrel more tightly and inched her finger even closer to the trigger.

Not where he wanted it to be.

She leaned forward, her brow raised. "Did you have anything to do with the man at the filling station?"

He took off his hat and raked his hand through his hair, trying to follow her train of thought. "What filling station?"

"Just off the highway. I stopped for gas and directions. A man followed me."

Some of the pieces were falling into place. "That's why you climbed the deer stand."

Her shoulders slumped and her eyes glistened with what he imagined were tears.

"Ma'am, I'd never hurt a lady. You don't have to worry. I won't hurt you and, if you give me a description of the man who came after you, I'll notify the local authorities."

"The Willkommen police department?"

He shook his head. "It's a county-run sheriff's department, although Sheriff Kurtz is in rehab, recovering from a gunshot wound. One of his deputies is holding down the fort, so to speak."

"Crime must run rampant on this mountain." The sarcasm in her reply was all too evident.

"You're not from this area?" he asked, hoping to steer the conversation onto a more neutral topic.

She shook her head but didn't offer a verbal response.

"Where's your car, ma'am?"

"Broken down on the side of the road not far from here. A warning light signaled the engine had overheated. I pulled off the road."

"That's when the man came after you?"

She nodded. "A few minutes later. I had seen him at the gas station."

"He followed you?"

"I'm not sure. He was headed toward the highway when he first left the station. He must have turned around."

"And he chased after you?" Lucas asked.

"That's right," she said with a nod. "I ran into the woods. He came after me and started up the deer stand. Thankfully, an animal rustled the underbrush and distracted him. He ran toward the sound, probably thinking it was me. Eventually, I heard a car engine and presume he drove off in his SUV when he couldn't find me."

Needing to gain her trust, Lucas pointed in the direction of the road. "You stay here and I'll check the roadway to make sure he's gone."

As much as he didn't want to leave the skittish woman, Lucas wanted to ensure the man had driven away as she'd suspected. He quickly made his way through the thick underbrush until he had a clear view of the roadway. A Nissan sedan sat at the side of the road. No other vehicle was in sight.

He returned to the deer stand. "It's Lucas," he announced as he started up the ladder, relieved to find her waiting for him at the top.

"I saw one car and only one car. A Nissan," he informed her.

"That's mine."

"Then the guy's gone. How 'bout we climb down the ladder? I can check the engine and see what's wrong with your vehicle."

She didn't respond.

"Unless you want to stay on this deer stand all night," he added.

The temperature had dropped even lower. Lucas could feel it in his leg. The wound had healed but the memory lingered. If the dampness bothered him, it had to be chilling her, as well.

Her jacket was light and her head and hands were bare. A slight mist had started to fall and she appeared to be shivering under her bravado.

"Not sure how you feel about a cold rain on a chilly night, but I'd prefer to seek shelter and stay dry."

Her shoulders relaxed. Evidently he was making progress. "I don't want to pry, ma'am, but you haven't told me your name."

"It's Hannah." Her finger inched away from the trigger. "Hannah Miller."

"Pleased to meet you." He hesitated before extending his hand. "Now, if you'll pass me the rifle, we can get out of the rain."

She sat for a long moment. Then, with a faint sigh, she handed him the .30-30. He checked to make sure the chamber was clear.

"I'll go down first. You follow." Swinging his good leg onto the ladder, Lucas started to climb down. Unsure how he'd handle the situation if she failed to move, he smiled to himself when she scooted to the edge of the platform.

"Easy does it, Hannah. One foot at a time. Take it slow. I've got your back."

The woman had been agile enough to climb up the deer stand. Surely she could climb down, as well. Still, he didn't want any missteps. Everything, including ladders, turned slippery when wet, and the last thing he wanted was any more harm to befall the pretty woman who had changed his plans for this evening.

In a flash of clarity, he realized her unexpected entry into his life could upset the peaceful existence he'd been living for the past eleven months. He'd turned in his badge, left law enforcement behind and found solace in the Amish community. Even more important, he'd gotten right with the Lord and found a simpler way to look at the world.

Savannah, Georgia, his years in law enforcement, and what had happened on that dock front were merely a memory. A painful memory that he chose to ignore. Except in the middle of the night when he awoke in a cold sweat, knowing his partner, Olivia, had died because of his delay in responding to her call for help.

He shook his head to send the thoughts fleeing then dropped to the ground and watched the woman with the long legs and free-flowing hair trudge down the ladder.

Her foot snagged on the second-to-last rung.

Without thinking, he caught her in his arms. She was slender and soft, and smelled like a fresh floral bouquet. He hadn't been this close to a pretty woman who tugged at his heart in eleven months and, for a long moment, he was transfixed by her nearness.

She bristled. He dropped his hold and took a step back, unsettled by the mix of emotions that played through his mind. A twinge to his gut told him getting close to Hannah Miller might be dangerous to his health.

"Are you okay?" He wasn't sure of the response she would provide, but he knew all too well that he was anything but okay. The woman had an effect on him that was difficult to define. Confused and befuddled might be accurate descriptions of the way he felt.

Gripping his rifle in one hand, he pointed to the trail that wove through the forest with the other. "The path will take us to the roadway near to where you left your car."

She swallowed hard and tugged on the bottom of her jacket before nodding. "I didn't realize there was a path."

"It's hard to see at night unless you know where you're going."

"Maybe you should take the lead," she suggested.

"Sure."

"You're positive the guy's gone?" she asked as if needing to be reassured that Lucas wasn't leading her into danger.

"I told you, your car was the only one I saw. You mentioned hearing a vehicle heading down the mountain."

Without waiting for a reply, Lucas started walking and was relieved when he heard her following. As nervous as she seemed, he wouldn't be surprised if she tried to run away. But then, where would she go? Her car was broken down, a man had followed after her, and she was halfway up a mountain road few people knew about and even fewer traveled.

He pushed back a branch from one of the saplings and turned to glance over his shoulder. "Are you okay?" he asked again.

"I'm fine."

The mist changed to a steady drizzle. Her hair was matted with rain that ran over her shoulders and down the front of her jacket.

"Fine" was a stretch. She looked cold and about as comfortable as a drenched kitten.

His heart went out to her, but then he realized his mistake. He knew nothing about Hannah Miller, yet a man had chased her through the woods. Maybe that was why Lucas had built the deer stand six months earlier. Had the

Lord placed it on his heart to do so, knowing a woman on the run would need a place to hide?

He was still a neophyte when it came to having a relationship with the Almighty. The Good Lord was working on making him a stronger believer and more willing to accept the precepts of the faith he had picked up from the Amish with whom he worked.

Thankfully, they had embraced him with open arms, but he was the one holding back because of the burden he carried in his heart. He'd asked God to send someone into his life who could remove the plank that weighed him down.

So far, God hadn't answered that prayer.

"Oh," Hannah gasped.

He turned to grab her arm before she tumbled over a fallen log. She nodded her thanks and leaned closer as she regained her footing.

His pulse hammered in his ears. What was it about this woman that caused him to take note? She was pretty. But lots of women were.

Maybe his protective nature had kicked into overdrive. Once a cop, always a cop, even after eleven months off the job. Still, he'd worked lots of investigations in Savannah and had never felt so engaged with a victim or a witness to a crime. Something about Hannah was different, and whether he liked it or not, he felt sure his life was about to change. For better or worse? Only God knew and, at the moment, He was silent.

TWO

Lord, keep me safe, Hannah prayed as she stared at the second man tonight who had peered into her car's engine.

"Shine the light this way," Lucas asked.

She angled her cell to where he pointed, grateful for the flashlight on her phone.

"Looks like there's a hole in the radiator," Lucas said, confirming what the horrible man in the flannel shirt had already told her.

The bad news was easier to accept from the helpful guy wearing suspenders.

She glanced at the road that disappeared around the mountain. A nervous tingle wrapped around her spine. The lewd guy who'd wanted information about Miriam could come back, especially if he expected to find Hannah huddled in her car, seeking shelter from the rain.

Lucas seemed oblivious to the danger. Although there was no telling what he was thinking with half his face hidden under that wide-brimmed felt hat he wore.

Swallowing hard, she gathered her courage to say what played heavy on her mind. "Do you think he'll come back?"

Lucas glanced out from under the hood of the car and flicked his gaze to the mountain road. "We'll see his headlights in plenty of time."

His comment lacked the reassurance she needed and wanted. Would they really have enough warning to hide if the man returned? Or could a car traveling at a rapid rate of speed surprise them both?

The Good Samaritan's nonchalance troubled her. Surely he wasn't in cahoots with the guy in blue flannel. She shook her head ever so slightly and sighed, refusing to go down that road. Better to think of Lucas in a favorable light. So far, he'd done nothing to cause her concern.

Besides, the Amish were peaceful folks. Weren't they?

Yet he'd said he was almost Amish. What did that mean?

"If we had some water, we could fill the radiator and drive until it ran dry." Lucas extracted himself from under the hood. "That might give us enough time to get to the B and B."

"Where you work?"

He nodded. "But as I mentioned, we need

water." He held out his hand, palm up. "And more than a sprinkling of raindrops."

"I've got a case of water bottles in the trunk of my car," she shared. "I went to the store after work—"

"And forgot to unload your groceries?" he added with a knowing smile.

Even in the darkness, she could see the dimples in his cheeks and the sparkle in his eyes.

"I planned to help with the youth at church," Hannah explained. "The kids are always thirsty."

"What changed your plans?"

She avoided his gaze. "It's a long story." One she didn't need to share. "Let's fill the radiator and see how far we get."

After unlocking her trunk, Hannah grabbed as many bottles as she could carry. Lucas did the same. He jimmied a tiny portion of cloth into the hole in the radiator, and then, together, they poured water into the reservoir.

"Looks like it's holding." He held out his hand when she pulled the keys from her pocket. "I'll drive. The roads can be tricky at night."

She liked his take-charge attitude and the smoothness with which he closed the hood, scooped the empty plastic bottles into her trunk and held the passenger door open for her. She settled into the seat and watched as he rounded the front of the car and slipped in behind the wheel.

The road twisted and turned, and she was grateful Lucas was driving. She glanced at her watch. Half past midnight.

Coming to an intersection, he turned right. A road sign pointed left to Willkommen. "Isn't that where I want to go?"

"The town is still a distance from here. The B and B is closer." He glanced at the clock on the console. "It's late, and you've got a radiator that's losing fluid. If we get to the Amish Inn, I'll be more than grateful. You can stay there overnight. The rooms are clean and comfortable and off the beaten path. You won't have to worry about the guy who followed you."

"How can you be sure?"

"I wear a lot of hats," he said with another smile that played with her heart. "One of them is security."

"But you weren't working tonight?"

"That's right. My shift starts at six a.m."

She hated to pry but another question came to mind. "If you don't mind me asking, how'd you get to the deer stand without a car?"

"I live in a house on the inn's property. There's a shortcut on the other side of the mountain. It's a good hike, but doable. When the parcel of land went for sale, I purchased it some months ago and built the tree stand as a place to go to be alone."

"Sorry I interrupted your serenity."

"Not a problem." He flashed another upbeat glance her way. "Glad I could help."

A comforting warmth settled over her. Then, realizing her error, she sat straighter in the seat. She wouldn't succumb to Lucas's charm. She'd been involved with one man too many. No reason to let herself make another mistake.

Lucas might be good-looking, but handsome men could break a girl's heart. She knew that too well. She had the scars to prove it. Not physical but emotional.

She'd built a wall around her heart. Unfortunately, she'd allowed someone entry and learned a very painful lesson that had forced her into seclusion over the last six weeks. Using a prepaid burner phone with a new number and changing her email address so he couldn't reach her had been good decisions. Moving to Macon and starting over had been a bit more difficult. Along with making a new life for herself, she'd fortified that wall around her heart even more. No one could find a way in.

Not even an almost-Amish guy with a killer smile.

Lucas tensed. His eyes locked on the rearview mirror and a muscle twitched in his neck.

"What's wrong?" Hannah asked.

"Headlights, coming this way. Looks like it could be an SUV."

"A black Tahoe?" she asked, rubbing her hands over her arms.

"I can't be sure of the make and model nor the color, but I don't want to take any chances." He glanced at the temperature gauge. "We can try to outrace the vehicle or hole up someplace and wait until it passes."

"What about the leak in the radiator?"

"You've got more water. We can refill if need be." Although putting extra stress on the car wasn't a good option.

Grateful when a narrow dirt roadway came into view, Lucas turned onto the path, guided the car behind an expanse of pine trees and cut the engine. "Hopefully we won't be seen."

"I'd like a little more reassurance." She tugged at a strand of her wet hair and stared through the trees at the all-too-close roadway. "What if it's the guy who came after me and he spots us?"

"Then we'll go to plan B."

Her eyes widened. "Is there a plan B?"

"Not yet, but we'll handle that problem when it arises."

As much as he wanted to make light of a very serious situation, Lucas knew cars on the mountain road were few and far between. Not that he would share that bit of information with Hannah. She was anxious enough.

"By the way, thank you for coming to my aid," she said, her voice barely a whisper.

He glanced at her for a long moment and then turned his gaze back to the road. "My mama taught me to be a gentleman, and gentlemen don't leave ladies at the top of their deer stands."

Out of the corner of his eye, he saw her shoulders visibly relax. She let out an almost-inaudible sigh of relief. As her tension seemed to ease, a tightness constricted Lucas's chest and sent a pulse of heat up his neck. He didn't have medical training but he doubted the reaction had any physical basis, and that worried him. Who was Hannah Miller and what was she doing to his peace of mind?

As the SUV passed, she touched his arm. "It looks like the Tahoe from the gas station. I told you, he had headed for the highway, yet when I broke down, his was the first car to happen by."

"The guy must have known you'd be stranded on the side of the road," Lucas said. "Did you lock your car when you went into the station?"

She thought back. "I had gotten out expecting to pay at the pump, then realized I needed to pay the attendant. I left the car unlocked."

"Which means he could have jabbed the hole in your radiator."

"Except I'd been driving for hours. The engine was still hot. Wouldn't steam and water spray out?"

"He could have worn insulated gloves to protect his hands. If he closed your hood before you returned to your car, you wouldn't have noticed the problem."

She nodded and stared into the night. "I went to the ladies' room, which gave him ample time."

"Did anyone tail you on the highway?"

"Not that I noticed."

Had the guy taken advantage of a woman driving along an isolated road late at night or was Hannah a known target?

"A pretty woman on a desolate back road…" Lucas didn't need to finish the thought.

Hannah leaned closer. "Did you hear about a mountain hijacking that ended with an older woman dead and two younger women captured?"

The question took Lucas by surprise. "How does that involve you?"

Maybe Hannah was a marked woman after all.

"The murdered woman was Leah Miller."

"You're related?"

Hannah nodded. "She was my mother. My younger sister Sarah was taken. Another sister, Miriam, was supposed to have found refuge with an Amish family named Zook. Do you know them?"

"That's a common name around these parts. Do you have first names?"

"Unfortunately, that's all the information I could decipher from the garbled voice mail Miriam left on my cell. The guy in the flannel shirt who came after me mentioned her name. He wanted to know where she's holed up."

"We need to talk to the deputy sheriff and learn more about the hijacking. Maybe he'll know the Zooks and how to find your sister."

Maybe he would know about Hannah Miller, as well. She'd gone from being a stranded motorist with a guy on her tail to a person of interest in a murder and kidnapping case. Lucas had distanced himself from law enforcement, yet crime and corruption seemed to have found him in the middle of the North Georgia mountains, which was both ironic and unsettling.

Reason told him to give Hannah a wide berth, but he couldn't walk away from a woman in need. Especially a woman whose circumstances tugged at his heart.

"Stay in the car," he said, opening the driver's door. "I'll add more water and then we'll be on our way. There's a fork in the road not far ahead. Just like the previous intersection, the fork to the left goes to Willkommen. We'll veer right toward the Amish Inn. Chances are good the car that just passed us is headed to town."

Lucas refilled the radiator, crawled back into the car, started the engine and pulled out onto the road. The rain eased, but the overhanging trees and thick underbrush that lined the road hung heavy with moisture. The headlights cut a path into the dark night.

As he guided the car to the right at the fork, the moon peered through the clouds. Stretched out around them were rolling hills that led to higher peaks in the distance. They drove in silence for some distance until fenced pastures marked their approach to the B and B. A three-story, rambling inn, painted white with black shutters, wraparound porches and two stone fireplaces came into view. The scene, no matter how many times he saw it, filled Lucas's heart with a sense of home.

"I'm sure everything will look more welcoming in the light of day," Hannah said.

Evidently the bucolic scene that warmed his heart caused her unease. She worried her fingers as if she didn't know whether to be relieved or concerned about what she saw.

"The inn sits at the end of the entrance drive," he explained, hoping to reassure her. "The building closer to the road is the Amish Store and produce mart. Fannie Stoltz owns the place. She's Amish and lives in one of the two houses at the far side of the property. The two Amish homes don't have electricity or technology. The rest of the property runs on solar power backed up with propane generators. The majority of the guests are *Englischers* who want to enjoy the peace of the Amish way but still have their comforts, such as indoor plumbing, electric lights, heat in the winter and air-conditioning in the summer."

"So it's not Amish?"

He smiled. "It's about as Amish as most folks want to get. Fannie is a widow. The inn was a way she could provide for herself."

"She has children?"

He shook his head. "But she's got a big heart."

"You're sure she won't mind me arriving this late at night."

"We won't wake her. I've got a master key and will set you up in a room. Tomorrow we'll explain your late arrival."

Lucas pulled her car close to a rear maintenance shed. "I'll have the mechanic check out your car in the morning. Calvin can fix anything. Even a radiator."

Rounding the car, he opened her door and then pulled her tote from the trunk. Together they hurried along the path that led to the inn and climbed the steps to the expansive front porch.

Lucas keyed open the door and stepped back to let her enter first. A small table lamp glowed halfway down the entrance hall. He placed Hannah's tote on the floor by the table and checked the log book.

"Room three is available," he whispered to keep from waking the other guests.

"Are you sure this is okay?"

"Of course. We all work together at the inn."

He grabbed the key off the peg where it hung and opened the door to the downstairs wing, then motioned her to the left. "It's the last door on the right, a corner room with great views."

He unlocked the door and held it open for her. She stepped into the room and flipped on the overhead light. Her gaze took in the double bed with fluffy pillows and hand-stitched quilt. A dresser and overstuffed chair filled one side of the room across from a door that led to the private bath.

A small latched rug warmed the floor, but the room was still chilly. Lucas adjusted the thermostat on the wall. "You'll get heat soon enough. Extra blankets are in the bottom drawer. Breakfast runs from six thirty until nine a.m. To get to the dining room, turn left and head to the end of the hall."

He stepped past her and checked the latches on the windows in the bedroom and bath.

"Lock the door after I leave. In the morning, I'll let Fannie know you're here." Lucas glanced around the room. "Do you need anything else?"

"Towels?"

"In the bathroom."

"Then I've got everything I need. Thank you, Lucas. I...I'll see you tomorrow."

He nodded. "I'll be on the job by six. Get some sleep. Morning will come soon enough."

With determined steps, he headed for the door then glanced back. "Don't worry. You'll be safe here."

Stepping into the hallway, Lucas felt a sense of relief. He had checked the windows and cautioned Hannah to lock her door. The guy from the gas station wouldn't find her tonight.

Once clear of the house, Lucas stopped to listen to the sounds of the night. Small creatures scurried through the underbrush and the croak of bullfrogs sounded from the nearby pond, but little else could be heard. No cars, no planes overhead, no chatter from guests who were hopefully enjoying their slumber.

He should have been relieved, but tonight something wasn't sitting well within him. He scanned the pastures and the mountains in the distance. Tired as he was, he couldn't pull himself from this observation spot as if everything was warning him to stand guard.

What had he overlooked?

"Gott," he said as his Amish neighbors did. "Show me through Your eyes what I am to see."

The night settled heavy around him, yet still he remained.

The light in room three, where Hannah stayed, went out. His eyes again scanned the fields, the outbuildings, the paddock and stable. A dog barked in the distance.

Foolish of him to remain for so long when the night was quiet. Ready to return to his house, he saw the glow of ambient light from afar. Headlights?

His spine tightened. Was it the man from the filling station? Had he taken the turn to Willkommen and then doubled back when he'd failed to find Hannah once again broken down on the side of the road?

The lights drew nearer. Lucas moved to the retail store and stood behind the building, hidden from anyone passing by yet with an unobstructed view of the road.

The vehicle's motor filled the night. Lucas watched a dark SUV pull toward the entrance to the property and slow to a stop.

He stepped from the shadows and hurried toward the car, bending to catch sight of the driver through the tinted windshield.

Although Lucas couldn't make out his features, he saw the driver startle, no doubt surprised to see someone approaching, before the late-model Tahoe accelerated. Georgia clay conveniently covered the rear license plate, obscuring the number. The left taillight was out.

The SUV passing the inn could have been anyone, except Lucas hadn't been a cop for six years in Savannah not to know the simplest conclusion was usually the best. Everything in his gut told him the man at the wheel was the guy from the gas station and, for whatever reason, he was intent on finding Hannah Miller. Was he interested in finding her sister Miriam? Or was he focused on Hannah? Whatever the case, one thing seemed certain. If the man found either woman, he planned to do them harm.

THREE

Hannah woke to the clip-clop of horses' hooves. She slipped from the bed and pulled back the curtain, then smiled, seeing a farm wagon stop at the side of the Amish Store. She checked her watch. Six thirty.

In the distance she saw Lucas hurrying along a path. He approached the Amish farmer. Together they unloaded boxes and hauled them into the store, then shook hands on the porch before the man climbed onto his wagon and headed back to the main road.

The sun was barely up, yet everywhere she looked groundskeepers and farm hands, many wearing typical Amish garb, were already hard at work. Dropping the curtain back in place, she hurriedly dressed and followed the scent of coffee to the dining area.

Entering the room almost took her breath away at the sight of the ceiling-to-floor windows that looked over the rolling hills, gardens and mountains beyond. Starched, white table-cloths and napkins dressed the round tables set with blue china that matched the curtains and made the room seem bright and cheerful.

A woman, probably midfifties, wearing a simple, calf-length dress and white apron approached Hannah. Her hair was pulled into a bun topped with a starched cap. Her round face and twinkling brown eyes were warm with welcome.

"You must be Hannah. Lucas told me about you." The woman took Hannah's hand. "I am Fannie Stoltz. I run the inn, and I am happy you can stay with us. Your room was to your liking?"

"Oh, yes, it was perfect. I slept better than I have in years."

The Amish woman's smile increased, and then she tilted her head. "Perhaps the reason your sleep is not usually sound can be worked out while you are here. The simple life sometimes lets us see more clearly that which is important. The world frets about too many things that should not have power over our well-being. Here—" She spread her hands and glanced through the windows at the rolling hills. "Here our focus can turn to that which is most important."

Finding her sisters was Hannah's number one

priority, but she didn't want to disturb the innkeeper with troubling thoughts of two missing women. Instead she chose a timelier topic. "You probably need my credit card."

The woman waved her hand. "We will deal with that when you are ready to check out. Now you must eat." She pointed to a table by the window. "You may sit wherever you like, but this is a nice spot. Lucas is mending a broken fence. Perhaps he will join you in a bit."

A young woman wearing the same garb as the innkeeper filled Hannah's cup with a robust coffee made even richer with the thick cream Hannah added to the hot brew.

"The cream is from our own dairy," the young girl said with pride. "You would like the regular breakfast or do you have dietary needs?"

Probably eighteen at the most, the server had alabaster skin and rosy cheeks that spoke of wholesome living. Even without makeup, the girl was beautiful.

Breakfast was hearty and delicious. Lucas never showed up and Hannah tried to squelch the disappointment she felt. Surely he would be on the grounds. She would find him there.

"Breakfast was wonderful," she told the server before leaving the dining room.

Hannah returned to her room and grabbed her jacket. Hopefully her car would soon be fixed so she could drive to Willkommen. She needed information to locate Miriam, and she didn't have time to while away the morning, enjoying the pretty scenery.

Opening the hallway door that led to the alcove, she nearly ran into a Hispanic man wearing jeans and a navy polo.

"Morning, miss. You are going somewhere?" he asked.

"Just for a walk."

He tapped the board where the keys hung. "You leave your key here when you are gone. The cleaning staff must make your bed and bring fresh towels."

"I wasn't thinking." She dropped her key onto the wall peg attached to her room number.

"You are the new guest?" he asked.

Hannah nodded. "That's right. I arrived last night."

"Someone gave me a note." He held out a folded sheet of white paper. "It is for you, yes?"

Seeing her name written on the outside, she nodded. "Who's it from?"

The man shrugged. "I know only to give it to the new lady."

Unfolding the paper, she smiled seeing Lucas's signature at the bottom of the page. *Meet me at the gazebo after breakfast. I want to show you around the property.*

Tucking the paper into her pocket, she thanked the man and hurried out the door. The musky scent of moist earth hung in the air and filled her with anticipation for the new day. She pulled her jacket around her shoulders and scurried to where Lucas had parked her car last night outside the mechanic's shed.

An African American man, midfifties with a lean face and slender build, greeted her. "I'm Calvin Crawford. You must be Hannah. Lucas said your radiator had sprung a leak."

"Sprung a leak" wasn't Lucas's assessment last night. Evidently he wanted to downplay what had happened. Not that she wasn't grateful. She didn't want to call attention to herself or to the incident on the mountain road.

"I'll have your car ready to drive within the hour, miss, if that works for you."

"Lucas assured me you could fix anything, Calvin."

The man laughed. "Anything involving motors or engines. Only wish I could do more to heal the human heart."

Seemed the mechanic was a bit of a philosopher.

She glanced at the various paths that ran through the property. "Which way leads to the gazebo?"

"Take the walkway on the left. It leads over the hill. You'll see the gazebo. It's not far."

With a quick thank-you, she hurried along the path he had indicated. Topping a slight rise, she smiled, seeing in the distance the lovely gazebo, painted white, with a curved roof and rimmed with colorful winter pansies. The setting would be an ideal spot to sit with a good book or to chat with a friend.

Although she didn't see Lucas, she continued along the path that led to a shaded area of trees and bushes. The thick undergrowth and tall poplars blocked her view of the surrounding pastures, the gazebo and the inn. The temperature dropped and even the overcast sunlight failed to reach into the dense, albeit well-landscaped, thicket. A gurgling stream ambled along the bottom of the steep incline. She walked to where a wooden walking bridge crossed to the other side. As peaceful as the hidden spot appeared, Hannah's thoughts fluttered back to the woods last night.

Her heart thumped and her pulse kicked up a notch. She wiped the palms of her hands along the arms of her jacket, all too aware of her body's reaction to the memories that played through her mind.

A twig snapped. She turned toward the sound. The world stood still as her mind tried to make sense of what she saw. A man. The same man from last night, wearing a hoodie covered with a blue flannel shirt.

She blinked, hoping to send the vision scurrying.

In that instant he started running straight toward her.

A scream filled the silence. Her scream as she raced over the bridge and up the hill. Rapid footsteps and his labored pull of air followed her.

Full from breakfast, she struggled to stay in the lead. The path wove through the wooded area and then into the open. She pushed on, seeing the pasture in the distance. Lucas stood, with his back to her, on the hillside.

"Help!" She flailed her arms and tried to get his attention as she kept running. Her lungs burned and she could barely draw enough air.

The guy was behind her. Too close.

His hand grabbed her shoulder. She jerked, trying to pull free, and stumbled forward. The path rose to meet her.

Air whizzed from her lungs as she crashed onto the asphalt.

"Where is she?" the man screamed. "Where's Miriam?"

He grabbed her arms and dragged her toward the underbrush. She tried to lash out at him, but the world spun out of control.

Lucas. He would save her.

Then she realized he didn't even know she was in danger.

Standing on the rise of the distant pasture, Lucas saw it play out in a flash. Hannah running along the path that led to the gazebo. A man following close behind.

Dropping his tools at the fence where he had been working, Lucas charged down the grassy knoll.

"Hannah," he screamed.

The wind took her name and scattered it over the hillside. He pulled his radio from his belt and called for help. "Mayday! Gazebo path. Beyond the bridge. A guest attacked."

He moaned, seeing the man dragging Hannah into the underbrush. Lucas increased his speed, wishing his legs would carry him faster. He cut across the clearing, screaming all the while.

Her attacker glanced up. For half a second, he stared at Lucas, who opened his arms and raced forward. The attacker released his hold on Hannah and disappeared into the woods.

Lucas hurried to where she lay and dropped to his knees beside her. Her forehead and cheek were scraped raw from the fall. Her breathing was shallow.

He wove his fingers into her hair, searching

for blood. "Hannah, talk to me. It's Lucas. Tell me you're all right."

Why didn't she respond?

She moaned and relief flooded over him.

"What…what happened?" She blinked her eyes open.

"Do you remember anything?"

"The man from last night." She grabbed Lucas's arm. "Where is he?"

"Gone. You're okay. He won't hurt you."

"But you said to meet you at the gazebo."

"What?"

"Your note."

Which he hadn't written.

"I was trying to find you, Lucas, but…"

She closed her eyes.

Fear tugged anew at his heart.

Her eyes reopened. "If he comes after me again—"

Footsteps sounded. She raised her head.

Lucas turned as many of the Amish men and women who worked on the property ran toward them, responding to his call for help.

Turning back to Hannah, he took her hand. "There won't be a next time. I promise you, Hannah."

Lucas thought of Olivia and realized the fallacy of his words. What happened once could happen again. Just as before, a woman was in danger, and if the attacker returned, Lucas might not be able to save her in time.

FOUR

Hannah appreciated Lucas's help, but she refused to be coddled and tried to stand as the workers flocked around her.

"Are you all right?" one of the men asked.

She nodded, but the ground shifted and her knees went weak. Lucas caught her.

"Easy does it," he cautioned. His strong arms provided support as a wave of vertigo washed over her.

"Thank you," she whispered, grateful for his help.

"You stood up too fast," he said.

"Fannie's coming." A workman pointed to the golf cart cresting the rise of the hill. Calvin was driving, and the innkeeper sat next to him on the front seat. They raced along the path and braked to a stop near the small crowd that had gathered.

Fannie hurried toward Hannah and wrapped her in her arms. "You are hurt. What happened?"

Lucas quickly filled the innkeeper in as together they guided Hannah toward the golf cart. Lucas helped her onto the back seat and scooted in next to her.

Fannie returned to the front. "Please, drive us to the inn, Calvin."

"I'm okay." Hannah tried to reassure them as the golf cart sped along the paved path. Her back and shoulders ached, and a wave of vertigo hit whenever she moved her head.

Lucas stared at her as if he could see through her attempt at bravery. She steeled her spine and blinked her eyes to block out the diffused rays of light that made her head pound all the more.

"You need a doctor," he announced. "As soon as Calvin fixes your radiator, we'll take your car to the clinic in town."

"It's almost ready to drive," Calvin assured him.

"The clinic is just off the square on West Main Street," Fannie said, her eyes filled with concern. "Doc Johnson accepts walk-ins, and the inn will cover any medical expenses."

"That won't be necessary," Hannah insisted. "I'm just tired and need to rest. I'll feel better as soon as I get some sleep."

"A concussion can cause fatigue," Lucas cautioned. "We'll let the doc check you over before any naps."

He turned to Fannie. "While we're in town, we'll stop at the sheriff's office and file a report about the incident."

"I am grateful for your help," Fannie said. "Will you also find out how Sheriff Kurtz is doing with his recuperation? He has been in rehabilitation for some weeks. I sent him a note that he should have received by now."

"Would he have information about the carjacking?" Hannah asked.

Fannie's brow furrowed. "I have not heard of this."

"A woman was shot and two women were taken captive more than six weeks ago," Lucas quickly explained, although he didn't mention Hannah's relationship to those involved.

Fannie patted her chest and tsked. "How can so much bad happen around us? This area used to be peaceful, which is how I describe the inn in the brochures. Now I am fearful for my guests' safety."

"I feel so bad," Hannah said. "I'm sorry to upset your tranquility here at the inn."

"I am more worried about you," Fannie assured her. "We must make certain this man does not hurt you again."

Hannah had left Knoxville and her sisters and mother in the hope of making her own way in life and finding a place to call home, which she was beginning to realize might never be in her future. She bit her lip and blinked back tears at the realization of what her future would most likely be.

Lucas must have sensed her upset. He circled her shoulders with his arm and pulled her closer, cradling her to him. "It's okay. The man's gone. I won't let him hurt you."

Hannah nodded her thanks and tried to smile. Lucas seemed sensitive to her needs and, at the moment, she needed the reassurance of his embrace.

Calvin pulled the golf cart to a rear door that led into Fannie's office.

"Let me help you," Lucas offered as he hopped out of the golf cart. Taking Hannah's arm, he supported her as she stepped onto the path.

As much as she appreciated his concern, Hannah didn't want to go to town. Willkommen meant traveling the road where she'd first been assaulted by the guy in flannel. She wanted to stay put at the inn. She would lock the door to her room and curl up under the hand-stitched quilt and sleep until she forgot about everything that had happened. But how far back would she have to go?

Memories assailed her of growing up and

being the odd child who didn't fit in. Her mother had told Hannah the truth about who her father was on the night she had left home. The same night her mother had accused her of being a thief. Hannah shook her head to block out the memories. She never wanted to remember the pain she'd felt. Better to be a woman on the run, trying to escape her past, than to open the door that needed to remain closed. Now and forever.

"I don't want to go to town, Lucas. I never should have come to Willkommen. It was a mistake."

"Hannah, you need to see a doctor. I'll stay with you. You won't be alone."

She stared deep into his brown eyes. Lucas didn't know who she was or anything about her family. What would he think if he knew the truth about her father?

She shrugged out of his hold, needing to stand on her own two feet. She didn't need anyone's help. If her mother had turned away from her, how could she trust anyone else?

Lucas didn't understand Hannah's need to be so independent. She seemed to change in a heartbeat, at first allowing him to help her and then backing away as if he was the one out to do her harm. She reminded him of someone who had been hurt, badly, and feared getting hurt again.

Lucas could relate.

Only his worst enemy was himself.

Hannah took a step forward. He reached for her elbow to steady her faltering gait. "The door leads into Fannie's office. There's a couch inside where you can rest and relax."

Her pallor had him worried, along with the lack of luster in her eyes. More than the wind had been knocked out of her sails.

"There's a small step." He pointed to the rise and held her arm as she navigated through the doorway and into the welcoming warmth of the office.

With Lucas's help, Hannah lowered herself onto the couch. "Thank you," she said, her voice little more than a whisper.

Fannie followed them in and drew water into a glass in the small sink at the rear of the room. "Take sips," she suggested as she passed the glass to Hannah.

"I'm really fine," she assured them both before she raised the glass to her lips.

Lucas returned to the golf cart to speak privately to the mechanic. "How long before the car will be ready?"

"Give me fifteen minutes," Calvin said. "I'll bring the car around."

"Thanks, Calvin. Let's keep this trip to town between us."

"You think someone at the inn might be involved?"

Lucas shook his head. "I'm not speculating on anything, but the fewer people who know Hannah's whereabouts, the better."

"Don't worry. You can trust me."

Lucas smiled. Calvin was a good man and an outstanding mechanic.

Returning to the office, Lucas was concerned by the worry he saw in Hannah's gaze and the lack of color in her face.

"We'll leave in about fifteen minutes," he announced, looking first at Fannie and then at Hannah. She must have realized her own fragile condition because she didn't object.

"My purse is in my room. I'll need identification and my medical insurance card."

"Stay where you are," Fannie insisted. "I'll get it."

She stepped out of the room and soon returned with the handbag. "Hector Espinoza is waiting in the hallway, Lucas. He wants to talk to you."

Lucas hesitated, confused by the request.

"Hector said he delivered a note to Hannah," Fannie explained. "He heard what happened and was worried he might be in trouble."

Hurrying into the hallway, Lucas spied Hector, hat in hand, a doleful look on his full face, and motioned him into a corner alcove that was out of sight from anyone walking along the main hallway.

"Who gave you the note?" Lucas quickly asked.

"The Amish girl who works in the store."

"Belinda Lapp?"

"*Sí*. She helps her mother."

"You saw her in the store?"

The man shook his head. "On the trail. She said you wanted the note delivered to the new guest. She described the woman. Belinda had shelves to stock, so she could not go to the inn herself. She said you told her that I would deliver the note."

"Was anyone with Belinda?"

"No, senor." Again Hector shook his head. "She was alone."

"Did you read the note?"

A look of surprise washed over Hector's full face. "I would never do that."

"But you found the lady?"

"She was in the main entryway. She is younger than the other guests. I did not have a problem identifying her."

"What happened after you gave her the note?"

"I returned to the barn."

"And Belinda?"

"I did not see her again."

"Thanks, Hector. You did the right thing in telling me. I know you were trying to help. Next time Belinda asks for a favor, talk to me first."

"*Sí*, I will do that. And the lady?" His dark eyes were narrow with worry. "The lady is going to be all right?"

"I think so. Now go on back to work, but don't let anyone talk you into anything again."

Hector left the inn through a rear door.

Lucas glanced out a nearby window to the store visible in the distance.

Why would an Amish girl be part of an attempt to do Hannah harm? Knowing she was in good hands with Fannie, he followed Hector outside and double-timed it toward the store.

A bell rang over the door and the smell of homemade soaps and fresh-baked bread accosted Lucas at the entrance.

Joseph, the Amish teen who worked with Belinda, looked up from where he was dusting shelves.

"Where's Belinda Lapp?" Lucas asked as he neared the counter.

"She has gone home for the day."

Lucas didn't understand. "The day has just started."

"*Yah*, but she did not feel well."

"And her mother?"

"She is not here, either."

"Both of them are sick?" Lucas asked.

The boy shrugged. "Both of them are not here. I do not know anything except what Belinda has told me."

Returning to the inn, Lucas pushed open the door and stepped into Fannie's office.

She was sitting next to Hannah on the couch, fanning the younger woman with a newspaper.

"What happened?"

"She got light-headed and almost passed out. She needs medical care, Lucas. Calvin parked her car at the rear of my office."

"We'll leave now."

He encouraged Hannah to stand and helped her outside.

Fannie opened the passenger door and wrapped a throw around Hannah's legs. "Lucas will get the heater running soon to warm you."

Before climbing behind the wheel, he hesitated for a moment. "Lydia Lapp didn't come to work today," he told Fannie. "Her daughter, Belinda, is the one who gave Hector the note to deliver to Hannah."

"I trust Lydia, but Belinda seems more interested in young men rather than in getting her work done."

"Have you seen her with anyone recently?"

"I saw her talking to a man this morning," Fannie admitted. "I told her that the store was open and she needed to get to work."

"Can you describe the guy?"

Fannie shook her head. "I was more focused on Belinda and her need to return to work."

"I'll talk to her when I get a chance. Hopefully she's not involved with the attacker, but stranger things have happened."

Fannie glanced into the car and patted Hannah's hand. "I will pray the doctor finds you well."

Hannah gave her a weak smile, which didn't bolster Lucas's spirits. He needed to get her to the doctor, but he also needed to talk to Belinda Lapp. Innocent though she seemed with her white apron and prayer *kapp*, the girl might know something. Lucas needed to find out what.

FIVE

Hannah disliked doctors as much as she disliked cops. Yet Lucas insisted on taking her to the medical clinic in Willkommen. The receptionist greeted them warmly before handing Hannah a pile of forms to fill out.

"I'm feeling better, Lucas," Hannah assured him. "You can leave me here and run errands or pick up supplies for the inn. I'll be fine."

He shook his head. "I'm not leaving. I want to know what the doctor has to say. Besides, I don't want you running out on me."

In spite of her aching head, she almost smiled. "Would I do that?"

He laughed quietly. "You look as skittish as a colt ready to bolt. You need to tell the doctor everything that happened."

"I'll tell him that I took a fall."

"That you were thrown to the ground forcefully, hit your head and have been woozy ever since."

"If I tell him all that, he'll keep me for observation."

"Which would probably be best. I'll be in the waiting room. Send the nurse to get me if you need anything."

The doctor was duly concerned about Hannah's condition when he finally entered the examination room more than an hour later.

"You've got a significant hematoma on your head, Ms. Miller." He glanced at her over the top of his bifocals and pursed his lips. "We need to make certain there are no complications before we decide how to proceed."

"I really don't think all the fuss is necessary."

"I'll order lab work and a CAT scan," the doctor suggested, "and go from there. Fortunately, a mobile imaging service is on site today."

Hannah knew arguing was useless.

The scan was painless and she was surprised to see Lucas waiting for her when she came back to the exam room. "I thought you would have gone to the sheriff's office by now."

"We'll go together as soon as you're released."

Four hours later they left the clinic with instructions for Hannah to rest. Lucas placed his hand on her back and escorted her to the car.

"You need to take it easy."

"I'm a guest at the inn. It's a relaxing place. I don't need a doctor to tell me to relax."

Except she didn't mention the man who had tried to do her harm. She wouldn't focus on that or on him.

"The sheriff's office isn't far," Lucas assured her.

"I'd rather not talk to law enforcement today."

"I know, but we need to notify the authorities about what happened."

She sighed. "What can they do?"

"Hopefully they can be on the lookout for the guy with a burned-out taillight."

The sheriff's office was small but tidy. A deputy greeted them. He introduced himself as Lamar Gainz and motioned for them to sit in chairs across from his desk.

Lucas took the lead and quickly explained about the attacker who had accosted Hannah last night and again today on the trail.

"Do you know the man's name?" the deputy asked.

"I saw him for the first time at a filling station." She explained about the hole in her radiator and how the man had stopped to offer his so-called help.

"He threatened you?" Gainz asked.

"His comments were offensive. I feared for my safety and ran into the woods. He followed."

"Did he hurt you?"

"Not then. Not until today."

At the deputy's prompting, she provided a description.

"And he was the same man who came after you today?" the deputy asked.

She nodded. "That's correct. It has something to do with my sister Miriam Miller. The man mentioned needing to know where she was. I'm hoping you have information about a carjacking she was involved in. My mother was killed and my young sister Sarah was kidnapped."

The deputy's eyes widened. "You're related to Miriam Miller?"

Hannah scooted forward in the chair. "I saw on a news report that Miriam left Willkommen. Do you have any information as to her current whereabouts?"

"You probably saw the clip about her boarding the bus. The local news station has run it frequently over the last few weeks."

Hannah nodded. "That's the one."

"Your sister left Willkommen but then returned to the area some days later. While here, she stayed with the Zook family, Abram and his sister Emma."

The deputy glanced at Lucas. "I doubt anyone at the inn would know Zook. He kept to himself. His farm is located a distance outside of town. From what I heard, Ms. Miller decided to join the Amish faith. I believe she and Mr. Zook planned to marry."

Hannah's eyes widened. "Are they at the farm now? I need to see my sister."

"'Fraid that can't happen. The carjacking was front-page news in our local paper and was picked up by radio and television stations in Atlanta. Lots of newsmen came to town looking for information. Abram was worried about Miriam's safety, so they left the area. Ned Quigley has been the acting sheriff while Sam Kurtz has been out on medical leave. Ned and Sheriff Kurtz are the only people who know how to get in touch with Abram."

"Then I need to talk to the acting sheriff," Hannah insisted.

"Yes, ma'am, but he's tied up at the Georgia Bureau of Investigations headquarters in Atlanta at the moment. Don't expect him back for a few more days."

"Give me his number and I'll call him."

The deputy nodded. "You could, but I doubt he'll divulge any information about their whereabouts."

"But Miriam is my sister," she reminded the deputy.

"Yes, ma'am, but that's the way they wanted it kept so no one could come after her."

"I don't understand."

"There's speculation a human-trafficking ring has been working in the area. When your sister's car was stopped on the mountain road, two men captured Miriam and her sister Sarah."

Hannah's heart thumped harder hearing her younger sister's name. "Do you know where I can find Sarah?"

He shook his head. "There's an ongoing investigation, but so far nothing has turned up. Your mother tried to protect Miriam when one of the men grabbed her. Guess Mom went after the guy. That's when she was killed."

"Would anyone else have information? Perhaps the sheriff who was injured?"

"Sheriff Kurtz? He's leaving rehab tomorrow, although I'm not sure where he's going after that. He needs to find a place to recuperate."

"Surely he has an apartment or home."

"Indeed he does, but that doesn't mean he can take care of himself. He'll need time to regain his strength."

"I want to talk to him," she demanded.

The deputy nodded. "I'll gladly give you information as to where he's staying once he lets me know his plans."

She raised her hands in frustration. "Can you tell me anything else about my sisters?"

"Only that Miriam was in good health and she seemed happy."

"Happy that our mother was dead and our younger sister kidnapped?" Hannah asked, unable to understand his comment.

"Happy with Abram, ma'am. Those two make a nice couple."

She wasn't convinced. "Are you sure my sister is safe with Zook? If what you said is true, Miriam might not be acting rationally. I never thought she would become Amish."

The deputy glanced at Lucas and then back at Hannah, making her realize her last comment may have been out of line.

"It's not that the Amish aren't good people," she said, hoping to walk back her comment. "But I can't see her settling down with an Amish widower, which is what she said he was on her voice mail."

"Abram's a good man," the deputy chimed in. "His wife died three years ago. He's had a hard time getting over her death."

"Can you assure me that Mr. Zook didn't abscond with my sister? For all I know, he could be working with the traffickers."

"Ma'am, Abram would never harm a woman."

"Yet he's keeping my sister's whereabouts secret."

"Which means the traffickers won't find her."

Lucas squeezed Hannah's hand. "We'll find out more information when we talk to the sheriff."

Although she appreciated Lucas's optimism, she still had questions. "Did Miriam say anything about our mother?" she asked the deputy.

"Only that she was sometimes hard to handle due to her ALZ."

Hannah leaned closer. "You mean Alzheimer's?"

"Yes, ma'am. Your mother hoped to reconnect with her sister. That's why the girls brought her to Willkommen." The deputy shrugged. "Sad part was that the hijacking happened before they ever arrived in town."

"I didn't know my mother had a sister."

"Annie Miller's her name, as I recall, although Miriam could never locate her."

"What about my mother's burial?"

The deputy frowned. "Sorry to say that, due to the murder investigation, her body hasn't been released yet."

Hannah's heart sank. "It's been more than six weeks."

He nodded. "With the sheriff in the hospital, things are taking a little longer."

A lot longer, she wanted to say. "Would you see when her body can be released? I'll make the arrangements."

"Yes, ma'am."

But not today. She wasn't up to picking out a casket or planning an internment.

"Where did the carjacking take place?" Lucas asked, changing the subject, for which she was grateful.

"A few miles past the Zook farm and the Beiler dairy. The road angles up the mountain to the county line. The Petersville police have jurisdiction on the other side of the county line. That's where your sister abandoned her car when she escaped from the cabin where she was being held."

"How far away was the cabin?" Hannah asked.

"A couple miles." He turned to Lucas. "An old guy named Ezra Jacobs lived near the road that leads up to Pine Lodge Mountain Resort. The two sisters were held not far from his place."

"What about Sarah?" Lucas asked. "Has anything been done to find her?"

"Here's the problem," the deputy admitted. "One of our men was injured in a vehicular accident the day Miriam's abandoned car was found by the river. He's been hospitalized in Atlanta since then."

"The accident was in connection with the carjacking?" Lucas asked.

"Not that we can determine, although nothing can be ruled out at this point. With Sheriff

Kurtz needing medical care and Ned Quigley at GBI, it leaves us short-staffed. We haven't received any leads for a few weeks. Miriam described the guy who took her younger sister as tall and slender with red hair. He shouldn't be too hard to spot, but so far, no one has seen him."

Hannah hung her head, thinking of the last time she'd seen Sarah, the night she'd left home. Her younger sister hadn't wanted Hannah to leave.

Swallowing hard, she glanced up at the deputy. "Please let me know if any information surfaces about either of my sisters. I'll be staying at the inn for at least a few days."

She turned to Lucas. "I'd like to visit the Zook farm and see it for myself, if we have time."

"Follow the main road out of town, heading west," the deputy told Lucas. "You'll see the farm just after the fork in the road. Two Amish lads, the Keim twins, are helping to maintain the property and livestock while Zook is gone. Tell the boys who you are."

He glanced at Hannah. "They don't have information about Abram or Miriam's whereabouts."

"What about Isaac Beiler?" she asked.

"His dairy isn't far from the Zook place. I haven't seen him or his wife and son for a few days. His wife's name is Emma. She's Abram's sister. I'm sure she'd like to meet you."

Hopefully Emma would provide more information and know how to contact Miriam.

"This case has all of us concerned," the deputy continued. "Plus, there was a young Amish girl who went missing some months earlier."

"Rosie Glick?" Hannah asked.

The deputy raised his brow. "You've heard of her?"

"Her name was mentioned on the late-night news report. She was thought to have run off with a boyfriend."

Gainz nodded. "That's right. Most folks think that's what happened, but when you've got a case like this with two women captured and another killed, you have to wonder if there's something we didn't see in the Glick investigation."

Lucas leaned closer. "Can you provide any more information about Rosie?"

"Only that she was seeing a young man in the area. A non-Amish guy."

"An *Englischer*?" Lucas asked.

"Exactly. His name was Will MacIntosh."

"You mind providing an address so we could talk to him?"

"Don't see how that would hurt if you can track him down. He left town the same time—that's why we thought they were together. His family used to live around here. The father wasn't the nicest of men."

"How old was Rosie when she disappeared?" Hannah asked.

"Seventeen. She would have had a birthday since then. The boy was three years older. The sheriff put out a BOLO on both kids but nothing turned up."

Gainz wrote directions on a piece of notepaper and handed it to Lucas. "You can talk to the girl's parents, although they might not be very welcoming. You know how the Amish stick to themselves."

He glanced at Lucas's clothing. "Sorry. I didn't mean to insult you."

"The Amish stick to themselves because they live apart from the world, Deputy. Not in the world."

"Sometimes their lives interact with worldly issues and that's when law enforcement gets involved, but that's something you might not understand."

Lucas scowled. Evidently he didn't appreciate the deputy's inference that someone dressed Amish wouldn't have a handle on law enforcement.

Hannah stood and shook hands with the deputy. "Let us know if you find out any additional information."

"I'll be in touch," Gainz said before they left the office and hurried to the car.

"There's not much to go on," Hannah admitted. Lucas opened the passenger door for her. "But it's a start."

He nodded and glanced at the sky. "Looks like a storm is rolling in. We can postpone the visit to Zook's farm until tomorrow when you feel a little stronger."

She shook her head. "I came to Willkommen to find my sisters. I don't want to give up now."

SIX

Storm clouds gathered overhead and rain began to fall as Lucas pulled onto the road heading out of town. He eyed the sky, concerned about the weather and Hannah's safety. Glancing at the rearview mirror, he checked for anyone who might be following them.

The rain increased in intensity. He turned the wipers to high and activated the defroster. Inwardly, he questioned his lack of common sense for exposing Hannah to danger that might lurk along the country road.

"We should turn around and head back to the inn," he suggested, seeing the stretch of isolation that lay ahead of them. "I'm worried about your safety."

"Don't be silly, Lucas. If I'm reading the GPS on my phone correctly, we'll be at the Zook farm before long." She stared at the screen, no doubt estimating the distance they still had to drive. "It would be a shame to turn around now."

Lucas flicked another glance at the rearview mirror. The road behind them was clear. The horizon was, as well.

"Promise me," he said, "that we won't stay long. We'll walk around the house, maybe check the barn, and then head back to the car."

"I told you, I just want to see where Miriam stayed. I won't cause a problem or dally too long."

"You're not a problem," he assured her.

She almost smiled. "Have you always been a worst-case type of guy?"

"What's that mean?"

"That you envision the worst."

"Seems you forgot that I found you hiding on the top of a deer stand."

She nodded. "Which I appreciate. I'm not sure what I would have done if you hadn't happened along."

"Knowing you, Hannah, you probably would have stuck a wad of chewing gum into the hole in the radiator, filled the reservoir from your stash of water bottles in the trunk of your car and driven to Willkommen to talk to the deputy sheriff."

"It was the middle of the night. The sheriff's office would have been closed, and I don't like to talk to law enforcement."

"But you did fine today."

"Because you were with me," she admitted.

"You've got a beef with police?" he asked.

"I'm a private person. Sharing information is difficult, especially with strangers."

"Your policeman is your friend. Didn't your mother teach you that?"

"My mother threatened me by saying she would call the cops."

The comment surprised him. "You were a difficult kid?"

"No. In fact, I was easygoing. I worked hard to help pay the bills and bring money into the family."

"But?" He stared at her.

"But my mother didn't believe everything I did was in the family's best interest. Deputy Gainz said she was suffering from Alzheimer's. That might answer some of the questions I've struggled with since leaving home. My mother hadn't been herself, only I was too stubborn to realize the deeper issues that must have played into her change of temperament. Unfortunately, I didn't see the signs. Evidently Miriam was more observant than I was, but then, that's what my mother had always said."

"That Miriam was observant?" he asked.

"That Miriam understood her," Hannah clarified. "They were cut from the same cloth, so to speak. Two peas in a pod."

"I think that's usually in reference to siblings. Perhaps you and Miriam were the two peas in a pod."

Hannah shook her head. "We were opposites. Growing up, I always wondered how we could be so different."

He glanced at her but she failed to divulge the reason behind her statement.

"The Zook farm's about ten miles from town," she offered after checking her phone again. She tried to appear upbeat, but he knew she had to be stiff and sore after the attack this morning and lack of sleep.

The rain eased and he turned off the wipers.

"It's pretty out here," Hannah admitted. "I can see why Miriam would have liked this area. She was more of a free spirit and loved animals and the outdoors."

"And you're a homebody?" Lucas asked.

"I'm content wherever, even a small apartment. Open a window and I have fresh air. I don't need to live on a farm to feel free."

"You think Miriam loved the freedom she found at Zook's place?"

"It's hard to say. Maybe she just loved Zook."

Lucas nodded. "You're right. Love can strike at the strangest times and places."

Hannah's cheeks flushed. She turned to gaze out the side window as if unsure of what to say.

He felt equally confused. Sometimes it was better to remain silent.

Hannah had said too much. Lucas had that effect on her. He made her see beyond herself and reveal details that had been buried for too long.

She jammed her fingernail into her hand, hoping to keep her focus on anything except the man behind the wheel. His eyes were too pensive as he stared at her and his questions too insightful. If she answered any more of his queries, he would know more about her than she had known about herself for all those years.

Why did it still hurt? She should be able to move on. Maybe it was her concern for Miriam and especially for Sarah that made her feel so despondent, as if she was wearing her heart on her sleeve. She needed to tuck her heart back in her chest, under her ribs and away from Lucas's penetrating gaze.

She didn't want anything to interfere with her quest to find her sisters, especially not a handsome almost-Amish guy who dug too deep and had a knack for making her reveal more than she should.

Glancing at the road ahead, she saw the farm in the distance. "That's got to be the Zook place." A white fence circled the property. A barn and a number of outbuildings clustered in the rear.

"Looks nice," Lucas said. "Zook's got a good amount of land. His pasture slopes up the rise where those horses are grazing."

He pointed at the other side of the main roadway. "Another farm sits farther down the road. That's probably Beiler's dairy. We'll stop at Zook's place first."

The gate was open. Lucas turned onto the gravel drive and parked close to the house. The home was newly painted and well maintained. Front and rear porches gave a welcoming touch to the two-story structure.

Hannah climbed from the car and hurried to the back door. Shielding her eyes, she peered through the window and into the tidy kitchen. "There's a woodstove, a table and dry sink."

Oil lamps sat on wooden wall stands, no doubt providing light for the entire kitchen. "It looks neat and clean and inviting."

Miriam loved to bake and, for a moment, Hannah envisioned her sister flitting around the kitchen, peeling apples and pulling pies from the oven, filling the house with the rich smells that made her mouth water.

Hannah was better with numbers. She'd kept the books for her family and paid the bills. That had been the problem.

Turning from the window, she stared at the pristine landscape, inhaling the fresh air mixed with the smell of earth and nature. She could see Miriam here, finding happiness and giving her heart to a good man.

"I'll check the barn." Lucas started toward the outbuilding.

"Don't leave me behind."

He turned and smiled. "Are you okay?"

She nodded, coming up beside him. "Maybe a little on edge after everything that's happened."

He held out his hand. "We'll go together."

She slipped her hand into his, feeling a warmth. Her anxiety eased and again she searched the landscape, seeing none of the threats and only peace and serenity.

"I can imagine that Miriam loved this environment."

"Can you see her in an Amish dress and bonnet?"

She shrugged. "Maybe. I'm not sure about her joining the faith, although she always begged our mother to let us attend church wherever we were living."

"You didn't share that desire?" he asked.

"Actually, I liked the services, the prayers, the sense of being part of a faith community." She smiled. "Plus, the people usually reached out to the little girls who came alone or with a neighbor."

"They probably tried to get your mother to join you in the pew."

"No doubt, but she always objected. Evidently her parents had been strict in their faith. She left home to get away from their control. Maybe their faith, as well."

Together they neared the barn. A rustling sound floated through the open doorway. Lucas stepped protectively in front of Hannah. Her heart pounded as she peered around him and stared into the dark opening.

"Well, look who came to say hello." Lucas laughed.

Hannah glanced down at a large dog with doleful eyes who stepped gingerly toward them, his tail wagging.

"You look like you've got a lot of Labrador retriever in you, boy. Are you all alone?" Lucas turned to Hannah. "Stay here. I'll check the barn."

Which made her concern return. "Be careful," she said as he disappeared.

She stooped to pat the dog. "You're a nice dog. What's your name, pooch?" She couldn't help but smile as he sidled closer and rubbed his head along her leg.

"Looks like we've got company," Lucas called

to her as a second dog scurried out of the barn. The beagle's coat was gray with age, but he was equally as friendly and enthusiastic as the Lab.

Hannah patted her leg to encourage the smaller dog to come closer. Tail wagging, the beagle looked up with big eyes as if begging for attention.

"You're as lovable as the big guy who shares the barn with you."

The beagle barked and then scurried toward the woodshed.

Lucas stepped from the barn and pointed to the dairy on the opposite side of the road. "We might find someone at home at Beiler's place."

As they hurried to the car, Hannah looked back at the Zook house with its wide porch. "In spite of what the deputy told us, I had hoped to find Miriam."

"We can come back," Lucas assured her once he settled behind the wheel and started the engine.

What would Hannah say to her sister if they found her? Their parting had been a painful memory she'd carried for the past three years. Coming face-to-face with Miriam would bring back the hateful words they'd both spoken needlessly. If only Hannah could go back and undo what was already done.

The drive to the dairy took only a couple minutes. Lucas turned onto the property and parked next to the house.

"I don't see signs of anyone." His voice was low and cautious.

"Two families couldn't just disappear."

He looked at the dairy cows grazing in the pasture. "Someone's milking his cows. The deputy mentioned the Amish twins who were helping Zook. The teens might be working the dairy, as well. Let's take a look around."

Hannah opened her door and stepped from the car.

Lucas headed to the house and knocked on the door. He glanced back at Hannah and offered an encouraging smile that she appreciated.

He knocked again then peered through the window for a long moment before he returned to the car.

"I'll check the barn."

A sharp wind blew from the west. Hannah shivered and glanced back at the Zook farm.

A buggy appeared in the distance. "Lucas?"

He peered from the barn. "Is something wrong?"

She pointed. "We've got company."

The buggy turned into the Zook property.

"It might be one of the Keim twins." Lucas motioned her toward the car. "Let's drive back to Zook's place."

The Lab barked as they once again parked by the house and hurried toward the barn. The young Amish man was pumping water that sloshed into the horses' trough, covering the sound of their arrival.

"Excuse me," Lucas said as they approached the youth.

The teen startled, surprise written on his narrow face.

"My name's Lucas Grant." He stuck out his hand.

The kid hesitated for a moment and then accepted the handshake. "You are not from around here."

Lucas nodded. "Not originally, but I've been working at the Amish Inn for the past eleven months. You might know Fannie Stoltz. She owns the inn."

The teen shrugged. "Perhaps my mother knows her."

"Are you one of the twins caring for Abram Zook's farm?"

"*Yah.* I am Seth Keim and my *bruder* is Simon." The slender youth gazed at the hillside. "You have seen my *bruder*?"

"We've seen no one," Hannah volunteered.

"I brought him here earlier before returning to town to help our *mamm* at the Amish Market. We have a stand. Usually my *bruder* and I both help, but the farm requires work."

"When will the Zook family return?" Lucas asked.

"This I do not know."

"I need to contact Abram," Hannah stated. "Do you have his address or perhaps a phone number?"

"The Amish do not have telephones."

"But you write letters?" she pressed. "Can you give me information about his whereabouts and whether a woman named Miriam Miller is with him?"

"I do not have an address. Isaac Beiler owns the dairy." Seth pointed to the neighboring farm. "You can see it from here. He would know how to contact Abram Zook."

"But Mr. Beiler is not at home. We stopped there briefly. Do you know where he and his family might be?"

"Simon knows. He talked to Isaac before he and his wife and son left for some type of a family gathering."

Hannah glanced at Lucas. "I guess we need to find Simon."

The big Lab trotted toward them. "What's the dog's name?" Hannah asked.

"Bear. He is Abram's dog."

"And the other pup?"

"The beagle is Gus. He belonged to Ezra Jacobs." Seth pointed to the road that passed the dairy and headed up the mountain. "Jacobs had a cabin not far from the road that leads to Pine Lodge Mountain Resort."

The deputy had mentioned Ezra.

Lucas stepped closer. "Have you been to the lodge?"

Seth shook his head. "Simon and I planned to look for work there, but it was closed for renovation. Instead we got this job. It is better to work the land than to clean hotel rooms." He glanced at Lucas. "I do not mean to insult your work at the inn."

Lucas smiled. "I handle the grounds and security, and agree with you about the benefits of working outside."

The young man glanced at the car parked near the house and the keys Lucas still held in his hand. "You are not Amish, but an *Englischer* dressed like an Amish man? This is what is done at the inn?"

"I'm learning about your faith, Seth."

"I have heard it is hard to leave your world and come to the *plain* life." The Amish lad narrowed his gaze. "Yet you look like a man who knows what he wants."

Gus raced up the hill, stopped on the rise and started to bark. Bear's ears perked up.

The Amish lad turned at the sound. "The dog has found something that causes him upset."

Lucas held up his hand. "Continue your chores. I'll see what's troubling Gus."

Hannah tagged along beside Lucas. Bear followed close behind. She inhaled the clear fresh air and glanced back at the pretty Amish home and barn, imagining Miriam walking along this same trail.

Approaching the rise, Lucas paused and patted his leg to divert the beagle's attention. "Come on, Gus. Let's go back to the barn."

"He wants you to see what he's found," Hannah said.

"Probably a dead animal. Maybe a squirrel or a rabbit."

She raised her hand to shield her eyes from the glare of the afternoon sun. Something lay on the grass. Larger than either animal Lucas had mentioned.

Her stomach roiled.

Not a rabbit or a squirrel or even a deer. Gus barked to warn them, not about *what* was lying on the dried winter grass, but *who*.

A young man. He looked almost identical to Seth.

Without doubt, they had found Simon.

SEVEN

Hannah gasped at the blood oozing from a gash to the teen's forehead. Lucas bent over the young man and touched his neck, checking for a pulse.

He turned to Hannah. "The kid's alive. Get your cell from the car and call the deputy. We need an ambulance and law enforcement. Now."

Heart thumping wildly, she ran to her car, passing Seth on the way.

She grabbed her cell from the console, tapped in 9-1-1 and tried to explain what had happened to the operator. "Send an ambulance and notify the sheriff's office. I'm at the Zook farm, about ten miles from Willkommen."

Hannah's head pounded and a roar filled her ears. What was happening to this idyllic Amish community? First her sisters had been captured and her mother murdered. A man had attacked

Hannah, and now an Amish youth had been left for dead.

Bear had followed her down the hill and now trotted to the rear of one of the outbuildings that, from the lumber stacked outside, appeared to be a workshop.

The dog growled then started to bark as ferociously as Gus had earlier. Seemed everyone, even the animals, was tense.

"It's okay, Bear," she called.

The Lab continued to bark. Edging closer to a pile of lumber, he showed his teeth and growled.

"What is it, boy?"

She neared, hoping to calm the distraught dog. "Did you see a chipmunk?"

Hannah patted her leg. "Let's go to the edge of the road and flag down the ambulance so they know where to turn."

Again she patted her leg. "Come on, Bear."

The dog wasn't dissuaded and continued to focus his attention on the lumber.

She stepped closer. A rustle sounded from behind the pile of wood. Fearing what she might find, Hannah turned, but not in time. The man in blue flannel raced toward her.

Her heart stopped, seeing his raised hand.

She screamed. The blow sucked air from her lungs. Her knees gave way. She heard Bear bark and then darkness took her to a place of silence.

* * *

Hearing the scream, Lucas ran down the hill. "Hannah!"

A man—the same man who had grabbed her this morning—was hefting her, like a sack of flour, over his shoulder.

"No!" Lucas cried.

Bear nipped at the guy's feet.

He yelled at the dog, dropped Hannah and ran toward the woods.

Lucas raced to where she lay, fell to his knees beside her and rolled her over, fearing what he would find.

His fingers touched her neck. He let out the breath he was holding once he felt a pulse.

"Hannah, it's Lucas. Can you hear me?"

A lump formed on her forehead near the gash from last night. She was taking a beating.

Her eyes fluttered open.

"Can you hear me?" He leaned closer, needing reassurance. "Tell me you're okay."

She grimaced, raised her hand and gingerly touched her head. "The guy's persistent."

Lucas almost laughed, feeling a swell of relief.

She lifted her head.

"Easy does it," Lucas cautioned. He placed an arm around her shoulders and helped her to sit up. "I'm not sure what the guy's after, but it includes you."

"He thinks I have information about Miriam. I wish he'd realize how little I know about my sister and her whereabouts."

She glanced up the hill. "Is…is Simon…?"

"He's alive. His pulse is weak and he's lost some blood. Seth is with him."

"What happened to the guy in flannel?"

"Bear nipped at his heels. When he saw me charging down the hill, he decided to make a run for it." Lucas pointed to the wooded area. "Last I saw of him, he was headed into that densely wooded area. Probably has a car parked nearby on one of the back trails."

"Help me to my feet, Lucas."

"Sure you feel up to it?"

She nodded. "I'll wait for you in the car."

Lucas wrapped his arm around her and helped her to stand. "Easy does it."

She leaned against him and rested her head on his shoulder. "I'm sorry to be such a problem."

He pulled her closer. "And I'm sorry I haven't been able to protect you."

The faint but shrill wail of a siren sounded in the distance.

After he got her into the car, Hannah squeezed his hand. "Flag down the ambulance. I'll wait here."

Lucas raced to the road and waved his arms once the ambulance came into sight. Two cars from the sheriff's office in Willkommen led the caravan and turned onto the property. Deputy Gainz and another officer of the law sprang from their vehicles.

"We've got two injured," Lucas quickly informed them. "The most serious victim is in the pasture." He pointed the ambulance toward where Seth stood waving his arms.

As the EMTs cared for Simon, Lucas told Deputy Gainz what had happened. "I'm not sure who attacked one of the twins, but the same guy we saw last night, wearing a blue flannel shirt, knocked out Hannah and was carting her off. If I hadn't come running, no telling what would have happened."

The deputy glanced at the car. "How's she doing?"

"Upset and maybe suffering from a bit of shock. You need to talk to her?"

"I'll have to get a statement."

While the deputy questioned Hannah, Lucas hurried to where the EMTs were loading Simon into the ambulance. "We're taking him to the hospital in Petersville," the head EMT told Lucas.

"How's his condition?"

"He's lost quite a bit of blood. I suspect the doc will order a transfusion, maybe two or three units. The lab work will tell more than our rapid screens here on-site."

"I'll meet you at the hospital," Seth assured the lead EMT. He hurried to his buggy and followed the ambulance out of the gate.

"The other deputy and I will stay and search the grounds," Gainz said to Lucas after he had questioned Hannah. "Watch yourselves getting back to the inn."

Lucas didn't need to be told. "If anything turns up, call the Amish Inn. Fannie will pass the message on to me."

"I wish we had more information on this guy. Ms. Miller is kind of fuzzy about what she saw, but from what you said about his clothing, my guess is the same guy is coming after her. She says she's got nothing that he wants, but he's got to want something."

"I think he wants her. If he was supposed to deliver Miriam to whomever the powers may be orchestrating all this corruption, he may need another woman to take Miriam's place."

The deputy rubbed his jaw. "Sounds like you know something about what's going down."

Lucas shrugged, not wanting to go into too much detail with the deputy. "I lived in Savannah for a bit. It's a port city. There was a trafficking ring in the area, but no one could determine who was involved. Except women disappeared. Girls from the street, mainly. Some younger girls, runaways. They were never heard from again."

Gainz stared at him with a questioning scowl.

"I read it in the local papers," Lucas offered as an explanation.

"Yeah?" The deputy raised his brow.

"That's right. I doubt this small mountain operation has anything to do with the Savannah group, but you never know. They use the port to get the women out of the country, maybe to the islands. The rumor was that one of the high rollers in Savannah involved in shipping had his own island in the Caribbean. There was speculation."

"That the women were being transported there?"

Lucas nodded. "You ever hear of a guy named Eugene Vipera?"

The deputy shook his head. "He's not from around here?"

"No, but I did a little research when I lived in Savannah and uncovered a trail that led to the lodge. I'm not sure if he's in a partnership or owns it outright."

"The lodge falls under Petersville police jurisdiction, so we never go up there. From what I've heard, it's five-star and top of the line. You have to have money and be well connected to stay there."

"Anyone from town work there?"

"No one I know. You could talk to the chief of police in Petersville, but you'd need to set up an appointment first. The guy's less than helpful. There was talk that a few of his officers might be taking money under the table, but nothing's been proven."

Gainz narrowed his gaze. "All it takes is one bad apple, if you know what I mean."

Lucas did know. Greed could corrupt the best of men.

Olivia? Lucas pursed his lips. Olivia hadn't taken the money as their chief had suspected. She'd been a dedicated officer of the law who had gotten too emotionally involved in the investigation, and she'd been set up.

Lucas glanced at Hannah sitting in the passenger seat of the car. Her face was pensive and drawn. She deserved better than what had happened to her.

He slapped the deputy's shoulder. "You let me know if you find out anything. I'll take Ms. Miller back to the inn."

"The attacker knows where to find her, Lucas."

Gainz was right. If Lucas took her back to

the inn, he was handing her over to the man in flannel.

But where else could she go?

Tensions were high as Hannah and Lucas left the Zook farm. She glanced back at the house where Miriam had lived. Her heart ached for Simon and his brother, Seth. The man in flannel was searching for Miriam, just as Hannah was. The Amish lad must have seen him and questioned why he was snooping around the farm.

Or had the attacker followed Hannah there? Had she been the reason Simon was in an ambulance heading to the hospital, his life hanging in the balance?

"You're not to blame for anything," Lucas assured her as if he could read her thoughts.

"Miriam and I parted on such bad terms," Hannah admitted. "Perhaps I shouldn't have come here today."

"Yet if not for your cell phone, Simon wouldn't have gotten the emergency medical care he needed."

"Maybe." Although Hannah wasn't convinced. Lucas thought more of her than she deserved. If he knew how she and her mother had parted, he would be less understanding and probably not as willing to help her.

She glanced at him, sitting straight in the

driver's seat, hands gripping the steering wheel. His eyes scanned the road ahead as well as the forested area that skirted the narrow roadway.

"You're worried." She said it as a statement rather than a question. The pensive furrow of his brow was evidence enough of his concern. "Do you think he's still hanging around?"

"The guy in flannel?" Lucas glanced at her for a long moment before he turned his gaze back to the road. "I'm not sure where he is or why he keeps coming after you. I'm wondering if it has more to do with you rather than just wanting to know your sister's whereabouts."

"Maybe if he couldn't have Miriam, he wants me."

"You mean as a trophy of sorts?"

She nodded. "For whatever reason."

"The deputy wonders if you'd be safer returning to Macon."

A heaviness settled over her shoulders as she thought back to the one-room rental where she had been holed up for six weeks. "Do you think that's what I should do?"

"No." His voice was firm. "I don't want you driving along the highway alone. The stalker's determined. I can see him following you south. You'd have to stop for gas or to stretch your legs. You'd be vulnerable. No telling what might happen."

She glanced out the window at the fading daylight. "I...I don't want to leave, Lucas."

"Then it's settled. You'll stay here."

"But he knows I'm a guest at the inn."

Lucas nodded. "That's the problem."

His shoulders tensed. Hannah felt the change more than she saw the shift. His eyes focused on the rearview mirror.

She glanced over her shoulder. Her heart lurched and a chill swept over her. "When did that car start following us?"

"It turned onto the roadway at the last intersection. The driver's probably headed back to town."

"We didn't pass anyone on our way here."

Lucas gripped the wheel even more tightly.

"Tell me the truth, Lucas. You're hiding something from me."

He shook his head and glanced again at the rearview mirror. "I'm not hiding anything. Let's see what happens when we speed up."

Lucas pushed down on the gas and the Nissan accelerated. Hannah's pulse thumped, seeing the vehicle behind them speed up, as well.

"There's a turn ahead." Lucas's voice was tense. "We'll take the roadway to the left that leads away from Willkommen and over the mountain to the inn. It's not a well-known route.

I'm sure the car behind us will continue along the main road to town."

Fear raced down Hannah's spine. In spite of Lucas's calming voice, she recognized the very real danger that could be following them.

The sun was setting over the horizon as they made the turn. The two-lane road was narrow and not well maintained. The front right tire hit a hole, causing the car to shimmy. She gasped and reached for the dashboard to steady herself.

"Sorry. Your car's not made for bumpy back roads."

Hannah glanced over her shoulder, hoping the car behind them would bear right. Instead it had followed them to the left and accelerated.

"He's behind us, Lucas. It's got to be that same guy."

"We'll be okay."

"We'll be okay if we can escape him. His SUV is larger and faster."

"The Lord will provide."

That was what Hannah had believed when she'd attended church in Atlanta. She'd met Brian and thought they had a future together. She hadn't known he was a thief.

Which was what her mother had called her.

Tears sprang to her eyes. She couldn't escape, not from the man in flannel who kept coming after her, not from the memory of her mother's hateful words, not from the mistakes she had made when it came to her heart.

"Night's falling," Lucas said. He glanced at her. "I doubt he knows the roadway."

The Nissan's engine chugged. She grabbed his arm. "What's that noise?"

"The engine's knocking. It doesn't like going this fast over a bumpy road."

"He's gaining." Hannah watched the car draw even closer.

The driver turned on his bright lights. The reflection flashed in Lucas's eyes, blinding him momentarily. He growled and adjusted the rearview mirror.

"There's no getting away from him." Fear ate through her gut. She clutched the console with one hand and the dashboard with the other, trying to steady herself as the car bounced even more over the pitted roadway.

A large hole appeared in the pavement ahead.

"Hold on," Lucas warned as he maneuvered the Nissan around the broken asphalt.

"We can't keep accelerating," she cried.

The last of daylight faded. Only the headlights were visible in the dark night.

"A small dirt road veers to the right around the next curve. We'll pull off there."

"He'll follow us, Lucas. We'll be sitting ducks."

The road ahead went dark as they rounded the bend.

Fear gripped her anew. "What happened?"

He didn't reply. Instead he made a sharp turn to the right. Tree branches scraped against the Nissan as it bounced along the narrow passageway.

Hannah raised her hand to her mouth to muffle her scream. The guy was right behind them, but all she could see was the darkness that swallowed them whole.

Lucas braked to a stop and grabbed her hand. "I cut the lights so he wouldn't see us. Pray, Hannah."

"Help us, God," she groaned, holding back her tears.

She closed her eyes, expecting the SUV to come up behind them. In her mind's eye, she could see the guy in flannel pulling both of them from the car. Strong as Lucas was, he wouldn't be able to save them.

Lucas chastised himself. Foolish of him to be traveling on a back road at nightfall in Hannah's old car. Why hadn't he realized the guy would follow them?

At that instant he saw the headlights of the SUV round the bend.

His heart stopped for one long moment, knowing if the guy turned onto the dirt path there would be no way they could escape.

Lucas had made a tragic mistake with Olivia. Had he made another mistake with Hannah, as well? One that would cost Hannah her life?

He squeezed her hand. Her slender fingers wrapped through his and held on tight, as if she needed him.

Olivia had needed him and she had died because of his inability to answer her call for help.

Lord, please.

The SUV passed the turnoff and continued on.

Lucas let out the breath he was holding. "It worked. He didn't see us."

Hannah gasped with relief then started to cry. "I...I was so frightened."

He pulled her into his arms. "I never wanted to frighten you, but it was the only way to get rid of him."

She nodded and sniffed. "It's okay. We made it. But what if he comes back?"

"We'll return the way we came and work our way through Willkommen to the inn. I need to use your phone to call Deputy Gainz and tell him we were followed. The cops are looking for a black Tahoe. Maybe they'll be able to apprehend him on that back road."

"And if they don't?" she asked.

"Then we'll find another way to keep you safe."

EIGHT

The night was black as pitch by the time Hannah and Lucas returned to the Amish Inn. Last night she had felt a sense of relief to find lodging and a place of reprieve after eluding the attacker. This morning, the hearty breakfast in the bright and welcoming dining room had wiped away the fear she had experienced the night before and made it seem almost like a dream. Then the vile man had struck again and again and again.

She glanced over her shoulder to ensure he wasn't following them now.

"He's not behind us, Hannah," Lucas assured her.

She turned back to stare at the inn, seeing the room where she had stayed. He had known she was there. He would know she was staying there again tonight.

"I…I can't, Lucas."

"What?"

"I can't stay here. He knows where to find me. Someone who works at the inn provided information about my whereabouts this morning. They could do so again."

Lucas pulled in a stiff breath. "It's late, Hannah. You won't find a motel for miles if you head south on the highway. You'd be vulnerable there, too."

"What if I just keep driving?"

"Back to Macon?"

To a one-room apartment furnished to a minimum with only a single bed, small dresser, table and two straight-back chairs. When she'd first rented the apartment, she'd been grateful for someplace to hole up, someplace cheap while she tried to elude Brian and find a way to survive. She was no longer worried about Brian but rather a new, more deadly threat.

"I'm not going back to Macon."

Lucas glanced her way. "Is there someplace safe you could stay? Maybe with a relative?"

She shook her head. "I've got no one except my sisters." Sisters who had disappeared.

He pulled into the entrance of the property but skirted the road to the front of the inn and, instead, drove along a narrow path that led away from the main lodging.

Two Amish homes, nestled on the side of a slight incline, came into view. She had hardly noticed them before due to a stand of tall pines that partially obscured the houses from view.

"Fannie lives here?" she asked.

"In the main house. She gave me lodging in the *grossdaadi* house."

"*Gross* what?"

He laughed. The sound filled the car and helped to ease the tension in her neck. "*Grossdaadi* means 'grandfather' in Pennsylvania Dutch. The Amish often build a house for their parents once they get older. The son and his wife help care for the aging folks, who are the grandparents to their children. Thus, their home is called the *grossdaadi* house."

"But Fannie doesn't have children."

"That's right. She bought the property after her husband died. The inn itself belonged to an *Englischer* and his wife. An Amish family lived on the adjoining farm with the two houses. After Fannie's husband died, she sold the property they had owned together and bought both parcels of land, the inn and the Amish farm."

"And made a success of the inn."

"The farm would have been difficult for a widow to maintain by herself, but the inn was a better fit. She had worked in the kitchen for a number of years and then moved into the other aspects of B and B management after her husband died. When the previous owners decided to sell the place, Fannie knew the opportunity was too good to pass up."

Hannah smiled at Lucas. "Evidently she also had a good eye in picking honest folks to work for her."

He braked to a stop in front of the larger of the two houses and turned off the engine. "I came here with a hard heart and a lot of anger. Fannie put me to work, knowing that physical labor would help diffuse some of my frustration. I had a bum leg and felt a bit useless."

He chuckled, as if remembering how needy he had been. "Fannie refused to coddle me. In fact, she was just the opposite. If I wanted room and board, I needed to do the tough jobs even if I was still recuperating from my leg wound."

Hannah didn't question him about his injury. Lucas was opening up and baring his soul. She wouldn't do anything to stop him from sharing a bit about his past.

"She was right," Lucas continued. "Work was what I needed." He patted his thigh. "My leg healed. My anger dissipated with time. Fannie's tough love helped me through it all."

"Which is why you've considered joining the Amish community."

He nodded. "They embrace peace. They're quick to forgive and don't harbor grudges. They rely on God—or *Gott*, as they say—

and they believe in hard work. Plus, they shun worldly ways."

He reached for the door handle before adding, "I've seen a lot of corruption and hardship and filth in my time. I started to believe the whole world was dark and evil. The Amish folks made me see how good people can be. That changed my life." He glanced at her. "Maybe the Amish faith could change your life, as well."

Before she could counter his comment, he stepped from the car and slammed the door behind him.

Hannah didn't want to be saved. Especially not by a sect of people who embraced the past. She didn't need the trappings of wealth or power, but she liked a few creature comforts, namely electricity, running water and inside restrooms.

Lucas rounded the car and opened the passenger door. "Let's pay Fannie a visit. I've got an idea about how to keep you safe."

"It's late, Lucas. I doubt she wants company after a long day at the inn."

He grabbed her hand. "Trust me, please."

"I do trust you, but I still don't think this is a good idea."

She stepped from the car and begrudgingly walked beside him up the porch steps. He could be insistent. Still, the calm peacefulness of the house was evident even on the porch.

Lucas rapped on the door then tapped again.

"She might be asleep," Hannah whispered.

Footsteps sounded from within the house. The covering at the window was pulled back and Fannie's round face appeared.

The door opened to the innkeeper's sigh of relief. "You have been gone so long that I had started to worry." Fannie looked past Lucas and reached for Hannah's hand, pulling her gently into the warmth of her home.

An oil lamp on the table bathed the room in a soft glow. A wood-burning stove sat at the side of the room, giving off heat.

"I feared some difficulty." Fannie narrowed her gaze. "What did the doctor say?"

Hannah smiled, hoping to reassure the woman. "That I need to rest."

"He kept you all these hours at the clinic?"

Lucas entered and closed the door behind him. "The doctor released her after a thorough check-over and a CAT scan. We had other stops to make."

"But it is dark now. You have been too long gone."

"We visited the Zook farm, where my sister stayed while she was in the area," Hannah quickly explained. "I had hoped to find information about her whereabouts."

"From the expression on your face, it appears you did not find that for which you were looking."

Hannah glanced at Lucas, unsure of how much to share with Fannie.

"We were followed," Lucas said, playing down what had happened. "I'm sure it was the man who attacked Hannah."

Fannie sighed deeply and patted Hannah's hand. "When will this end?"

Hannah felt the burden fall heavy on her shoulders. "I've placed you and your guests in danger, Fannie. I'm so sorry."

"Oh, child. You are not at fault. You have done nothing wrong. It is this man who comes after you."

Fannie glanced at her watch. "It is late. You have eaten?"

"We hurried to get back to the inn and failed to stop," Lucas said. "Is the dining room still open?"

"Not this late, but I will fix food to fill your stomachs."

"There's something else we need," Lucas added. "The man knows Hannah rented a room at the inn. She has no other place to go, yet she needs to remain in the area until she can find her sisters."

Lucas explained that Hannah's family had been the victims of the carjacking and the tragedy that ensued. "Which means she needs a safe place to stay where the assailant won't find her."

"Here," Fannie suggested immediately. She turned to Hannah. "You will stay with me. He will never expect to find you in an Amish home."

She looked at Hannah's jeans and jacket. "Those who work at the inn wear nothing fancy, but we can do even more to protect you. You will dress in true Amish clothing."

"You mean like Lucas?"

"That's right, except you will wear a dress, apron and bonnet. The attacker will never look for you among the Amish. What do you think?"

Hannah glanced down at her clothes and then at what Fannie was wearing. "I think that sounds like a good plan."

The next morning Hannah awoke with a start. She glanced at the quilt that covered her and turned to stare at the pegs on the wall where a dress hung, along with a white apron.

For a moment she couldn't get her bearings. Then everything flooded back to her. She was in Fannie's house, an Amish house with simple, no-fuss furnishings.

Pulling back the bed coverings, she dropped her feet to the hardwood floor and shivered in the chill of the room.

Her own clothing lay on a small straight-back chair. She passed them by and reached instead for the cotton dress hanging from the peg. She hesitated for a moment, questioning her own wisdom about taking on a way of life about which she knew so little.

The assailant's hateful face floated through her thoughts and wiped away any indecision about dressing Amish.

Quickly she donned the blue frock and reached for the straight pins Fannie had left on a side table. Feeling all thumbs and clueless about how she could hold the fabric together, Hannah breathed a sigh of relief when she heard a knock at the door and Fannie's cheerful *"Gude mariye"* from the hallway.

"Breakfast is almost ready," the older woman said.

Hannah cracked open the door and invited her into the bedroom. Fannie dropped the small suitcase she carried in the corner. "Lucas brought your things from the inn this morning."

"That was thoughtful of him." Hannah pointed to the waistband she held together with her other hand. "But right now, I need your help, Fannie. I'm all thumbs when it comes to pinning the fabric."

The woman's laughter filled the room with warmth as she tugged on the waistband and quickly worked the pins through the layers of fabric.

"The trick is to make certain the tips of the pins are buried within the thickness of the cloth so you do not catch your hand against the sharp tips."

"I don't know how you do it." Hannah ran her hand over the pins that now held the dress together as securely as a row of buttons.

"Practice makes perfect, as the saying goes. You will soon learn many of the Amish ways." Fannie's smile touched a lonely place within Hannah's heart. "The Amish leave the world behind and embrace hard work and love of *Gott*. *All things work together*, as scripture reminds us. You will remember this?"

"I'm afraid there's too much to learn," Hannah admitted. Once again she ran her hand over the row of pins. Would she ever be able to dress herself let alone learn the many tenets of the Amish life?

Fannie reached for the apron and slipped it over Hannah's head. Standing back, she nodded in approval. "*Yah*, you look like one of us."

Hannah carried too many struggles within her to be Amish. Most especially the animosity she still harbored, remembering her mother's verbal attack the night she'd left home. The night she had learned the truth about her father and the type of man he was.

Hannah had always been the outsider. Growing up, she had questioned her mother's caustic comments about her first child being born out of pain. That night Hannah had better understood her mother's all-too-frequent criticism.

"What is it, Hannah?" Fannie touched her arm and smiled with understanding. "You are remembering something that troubles you?"

She nodded. "I'm thinking of my youth. I… I grew up in a chaotic home. Love—if it was even that—had to be earned. I never seemed to do what was right."

Fannie nodded. "Perhaps *Gott* has brought you here to sort out the past. Painful memories can be like a millstone around our necks, unless we are able to cut free from that which weighs us down. Not all homes are built on love. My own home growing up was filled with turmoil. When I married Eli, I vowed our children would know love and acceptance and not harsh unforgivingness."

"But I thought all Amish homes were filled with peace and understanding."

"That is the ideal for which we strive. Sometimes people fall short of the ideal."

"Lucas said you didn't have children."

Fannie smiled. "One son. He died as an infant. I blamed *Gott* for too long. My husband was gentle and loving. He understood that we must accept what *Gott* wills for our lives."

"But God didn't want your child to die, Fannie."

"He did not. This I had to learn. Eventually, I realized I had to accept life as it was. That millstone I mentioned weighed me down until I could forgive *Gott* and myself."

"And you had no more children?"

"I have Lucas. He came into my life. He, too, was broken. I consider him the son *Gott* took from me."

"You were given a second chance."

Fannie tilted her head. "Are you longing for that, as well?"

Hannah shrugged her shoulders. "Growing up, I never fit in. My mother found fault, more with me than with my sisters. I worked to help support the family, but I also saved some of my earnings and kept the cash in my bottom drawer."

Although she hadn't expected to bare her heart, the understanding she saw in Fannie's gaze made her give voice to that which she had kept hidden for too long. "Three years ago, I decided to count my savings only to find the money gone. I... I confronted my mother."

Hannah's heart pounded, remembering the argument that had ensued. "My mother said the money belonged to the family even though I had earned it working overtime. She called me a thief. She said I had stolen from the family and threatened to turn me over to the police."

"Oh, child." Fannie opened her arms and pulled Hannah into a loving embrace. "You are not a thief. You are a beautiful young woman, yet you grieve not only for your mother but also for the love that perhaps she could not provide."

What Fannie had said was true. Hannah had grieved the loss of her family for so long. Had God brought her here to heal?

"Thank you for the clothes and for letting me stay with you, Fannie."

"You are safe with me, child. We will think of happy thoughts and not allow the past to cloud our sunshine. *Yah?*"

Hannah laughed through her tears, feeling a sense of homecoming and wholeness. *"Yah."*

Fannie handed her a handkerchief. "Wipe your eyes and then we will go downstairs and have breakfast together. I must leave soon for the inn. You can decide what you will do today."

Hannah followed Fannie into the kitchen,

where the table was set for three. Fannie quickly pulled biscuits from the woodstove's oven and piled them in a basket that she placed on the table.

A cast-iron skillet on a back burner contained scrambled eggs. A plate of bacon, crisp and succulent, warmed there, as well.

"May I pour coffee?" Hannah asked.

"Many hands make light work," Fannie said with a definitive nod.

Hannah poured the pungent brew into two cups on the table and then turned, holding the pot in midair, back to Fannie. "Shall I fill a cup for Lucas?"

As if on cue, the kitchen door opened and he stepped inside, bringing with him the clean scent of fresh air. "Morning, ladies." His face warmed with a wide smile and twinkling eyes that made Hannah's heart flutter.

"I'll take a cup of that coffee," he said as he hung his waistcoat and hat on a peg by the door.

Hannah poured the coffee and handed him the sturdy cup. Their fingers touched and he gazed into her eyes. "Smells wonderful."

"You've been working?" she asked, suddenly flustered and unsure of her voice as well as her heart.

"I wanted to check the fence I fixed yesterday." He glanced at Fannie. "No one bothered it last night, but it didn't come down by accident. I fear the man who attacked Hannah wanted to create a distraction."

"Having the cattle break out of the pasture would have been a distraction for certain."

"But the broken fence forced you to be in the pasture when I needed help." Hannah voiced what she knew to be true. "You rescued me, Lucas."

"*Gott* provides when we are in need." Fannie motioned them to the table.

Lucas held a chair for Hannah and then sat across from her and bowed his head.

"We will give thanks." Fannie followed Lucas's lead.

Hannah did, as well. The innkeeper's heartfelt prayer filled Hannah with a sense of well-being in spite of everything that had happened. Glancing up after the prayer ended, she was taken aback by the overwhelming contentment that swept over her.

Her whole life she had longed for stability and love. For some strange reason, she had found it—at least for this moment in time—in an Amish home in the North Georgia mountains.

Was that what Miriam had found at the Zook farm? Was that why she had fallen in love with an Amish man who had, more than likely, disavowed the ways of the world?

Hannah glanced at Lucas. He stopped his fork, filled with eggs, midway to his mouth and gazed at her across the table. What she saw in his eyes warmed her. Understanding, acceptance, concern.

Had she stumbled onto the very place for which she had been searching?

She clenched her left hand on her lap and reached for her coffee with her right as her thoughts returned to the reality of her plight.

She had allowed a man access to her heart before but he had lied to her. She was too much like her mother, giving her heart to someone who wasn't the man she thought him to be.

Surely Fannie was an excellent judge of character, and if she loved Lucas like a son, then he had to be a good man.

But Brian had seemed like a good man, too.

Hannah had learned the truth, which had made her realize how gullible she really had been. She wouldn't make the same mistake again.

Suddenly, Hannah wasn't hungry. She was worried. Worried about the man who kept coming after her, worried about staying in an Amish home with a woman she had only just met, and worried about feelings of attraction for the man sitting across the table from her.

Hannah knew so little about her biological father but she knew her deceased mother too well. Unfortunately, she was and would always be her mother's daughter. Shame on her. Hannah needed to guard her heart and her life. Staying at the Amish Inn was probably a mistake. Hopefully one she wouldn't come to regret.

NINE

Lucas didn't want breakfast to end. Sitting across from Hannah warmed his heart and lightened the burden he had carried since Olivia's death. He hadn't thought a meal could be so enjoyable, and it wasn't due to Fannie's excellent cooking. He had sat at this very table eating the wonderful food she provided many a morning without feeling the buoyancy to his spirits that filled him today.

Hannah stared at her plate, which provided Lucas a moment to study her pretty features. He had been attracted to her oval face and crystal-blue eyes the night they'd met. Yet seeing her this morning with her hair pulled back in a bun and wearing the white *knapp*, or bonnet, made him see the deep beauty, the true beauty, she possessed.

He doubted many *Englisch* women would be comfortable without their makeup and hair products, thinking their looks would diminish without the accoutrements. Hannah, on the other hand, had grown in grace and poise and seemed to have an inner glow he hadn't noticed earlier. Even the bruises on her forehead and the scrape on her cheek seemed better today.

"Calvin fixed the wheel on one of the buggies," Lucas informed both women. "I want to make sure it won't give anyone a problem and thought I'd take it for a ride this morning."

Fannie nodded. "That sounds like a good idea. Where are you planning to go?"

"I thought about heading to the Glicks' home. It's not far if I go along the back path."

"Rosie Glick?" Hannah asked. "The Amish girl who ran off with her *Englisch* boyfriend?"

"That's right." Lucas nodded. "She disappeared three months after I came to Willkommen. At the time, I didn't think much about it."

"Such a thing has happened before," Fannie admitted. "Young girls taken in by non-Amish men who promise them all the world offers. My heart breaks for the families torn apart when their children reject the faith."

"Are the girls shunned?" Hannah asked.

"If they have been baptized and have already accepted the Amish faith, then, *yah*, they are shunned by their families and their communities if they leave the order."

"That sounds harsh."

Fannie gazed with understanding at Hannah. "Does it seem harsh? The one who leaves does not desire what we have within the Amish faith. They are the ones who turn their backs on us. We cannot open ourselves to more pain by those who do not wish to follow the *Ordnung*."

"The rule that guides each Amish community," Lucas explained.

"A mother always knows her child," Fannie continued. "Yet in these cases, the child has turned his or her back on the mother first. Repentance can be achieved. The one who left confesses the wrongdoing to the bishop and the church, and asks forgiveness."

"You mean they can gain acceptance into the community again?" Hannah asked.

"It is possible."

"So Rosie could come back?"

"If that is her desire and if she is willing to confess her actions and ask forgiveness."

"But—" Hannah looked at Lucas. "There's something you're not telling me."

"Lucas has come to feel the way I do about this girl," Fannie volunteered. "Something more is at stake here. Rosie was an impressionable young woman. She believed her heart about a young man who perhaps lied to her."

Lucas saw the pain fill Hannah's gaze as if she was all too aware of how that could happen. Was she reflecting on her own mother? Or on her own life?

"Fannie fears that harm may have come to Rosie Glick." Lucas said what he and Fannie both believed to be true.

"You're talking about foul play?"

He nodded.

"That's what the television reporter mentioned. They said law enforcement is looking anew at her disappearance."

Hannah lowered her fork. "I wish someone had information about my youngest sister. If what people have said about Abram Zook is true, Miriam may no longer be in danger. But Sarah? She's only twenty-one. I haven't seen her for three years. At that time she was so sweet and too naive. I don't know if she would have the stamina to survive."

"Yet you said your upbringing was not good," Fannie added. "She survived growing up, which may give her the stamina and determination to survive other challenges."

"I hope you're right, Fannie."

The older woman patted Hannah's hand. "We will trust *Gott, yah?*"

Hannah nodded and then turned to Lucas. "Take me with you when you talk to the Glick family. They might know something that could help me find Sarah."

"The man came after you, Hannah. Stay here where you'll be safe. I'll let you know what I learn."

She shook her head and grabbed his hand. "The attacker is looking for a woman in jeans and a jacket. He won't be looking into Amish buggies."

"He saw me run toward him yesterday," Lucas reminded her. "I don't want to draw his attention, especially if we're together."

Hannah smiled. "But he wouldn't be looking for an Amish couple. You'll be safer with me than if you went alone."

"I'm not worried about myself. I'm worried about you. Besides, it'll be a cold trip," he cautioned.

"Surely Fannie has a coat I could wear."

"A cape," the older woman volunteered, "and a large black bonnet with a brim that will hide your face if anyone happens by who seems unfriendly."

She patted Hannah's hand. "You are right. The man in flannel will not be looking for an Amish couple riding in a buggy."

"But—" Lucas didn't like putting Hannah in danger, even if she was hiding undercover in Amish clothing. He didn't know much about the attacker, but he knew that the man kept coming after Hannah. Would he follow them to the

Glick farm? If so, would Lucas be able to keep Hannah safe?

He had left law enforcement and didn't want to return to that way of life, but everything had changed when he'd found Hannah on the deer stand.

She needed to find her sisters, especially Sarah. If the local deputy wasn't able to carry out the investigation, Lucas couldn't sit by and do nothing. Even if returning to police work was the last thing he wanted for his life.

A young woman was missing. An Amish girl had disappeared. Lucas needed to determine if there was a connection.

Fannie was right. The attacker wouldn't recognize Hannah in the blue dress and white apron. He was looking for an attractive woman of the world instead of a pretty Amish gal with a scrubbed face and piercing blue eyes.

"All right. We'll go together. I'll hitch the mare to the buggy. Be sure to wear the bonnet and cape when you step outside. I'll bring the buggy to the kitchen door." He glanced at Fannie. "No one is to know about your visitor."

"She's a niece from Tennessee, if anyone asks." Fannie patted Hannah's hand. "I'm accepting you as kin right here and now. You are family to me." The older woman glanced across the table to Lucas. "You are family, as well, Lucas."

The words touched his heart.

She glanced back at Hannah. "And this sweet Amish woman is the niece I never knew who has only recently come into my life."

Hannah's eyes filled with tears. Evidently she was as touched as Lucas. Fannie had a big heart. She should have had a houseful of children and grandchildren, yet that was not the path God had chosen for her life.

"I'll get the buggy." Lucas rose from the table and, without saying anything else, shrugged into his waistcoat, situated his hat on his head and left the warmth of the kitchen.

A cold wind whipped around the house and tugged at his jacket. Lucas lowered his face into the wind and walked toward the barn. What would they find today at the Glick house?

He didn't know. The only thing he did know was that a man was after Hannah. And Lucas—even though he had left law enforcement—needed to keep her safe. He touched his hip where he had carried a weapon for years. Unarmed and wanting to be Amish didn't make for a good combination when evil prowled. Lucas would have to be extra cautious and use all his skills to make sure Hannah didn't end up in the wrong place at the wrong time.

"*Gott* help me," he quietly prayed. Perhaps

if the Lord realized his desire to live the *plain* life, He would keep them both safe.

That was Lucas's hope. He glanced back at the kitchen and saw Hannah gazing at him through the window. What was she thinking? Was she thinking about her sister Sarah or about the wannabe Amish man who didn't understand his own heart?

Hannah slipped into the black cape and bonnet that Fannie offered, grateful for the older woman who adjusted the bonnet and tied the ribbons under Hannah's chin.

"No one will recognize you," Fannie assured her. Then, peering out the kitchen window, she motioned her toward the door. "Lucas is bringing the buggy."

Hannah stepped onto the porch, feeling the warmth of the heavy cape and enjoying the way the dress moved with her. The clothing she thought would be encumbering turned out to be freeing. She also liked the smile of appreciation Lucas flashed her way before he helped her into the buggy.

He sat next to her and flicked the reins, urging Daisy forward.

Once they passed the Amish Store and turned onto the main road, Lucas settled back in the seat. "Belinda Lapp is the young woman who works at the store. She gave Hector the note yesterday that he passed on to you. The Lapp farm isn't far. I want to stop there first."

But no one answered the door when Lucas knocked. He checked the barn and the pastures before returning to the buggy.

"Seems all the families in this area have left their farms," Hannah mused, hoping to deflect his frustration.

"They might be in town," he admitted. "Many of the folks sell produce and baked goods at the Amish Market in Willkommen. Lydia is known for her jellies and jams as well as the quilts she stitches. Too frequently, the Amish around here need to supplement their incomes. I'm sure the Lapps could use the extra cash."

"We'll come back again," Hannah suggested.

He nodded and hurried Daisy along. They rode in silence while Hannah thought of the young Amish women trying to find their way and be true to their faith in a world filled with enticements.

"I don't have a good feeling about Rosie Glick." She finally shared what had been bothering her, knowing Lucas and Fannie felt a similar unease. "Why would an Amish girl run off with an *Englischer*?"

Lucas shrugged. "The grass looks greener, as the saying goes. She might have struggled with her own parents. The Amish life isn't easy and the lure of the world can be enticing, especially for a teenager. The Glick farm isn't far. Let's stop there first and then head to the boyfriend's place after we talk to Rosie's parents."

"That sounds good."

"But we need to be careful," he added. "The guy in blue flannel is still on the loose."

Lucas seemed genuinely concerned for her safety, which made Hannah feel special. A feeling she'd never experienced around men. Initially the guy she had dated in Atlanta had been considerate of her feelings, but he'd soon changed and put his own desires first. Thankfully, she'd found out the truth about who he really was before it was too late.

"You're quiet." Lucas interrupted her thoughts. "Everything okay? You're not feeling sick, are you?"

She shook her head. "I'm just musing over what's happened. I never thought a fast trip to Willkommen to reconnect with my sisters would put me in danger."

"Nothing like this has happened before?"

She didn't like his question. "Are you suspicious?"

"Of you?"

"That I might have brought this upon myself."

He shook his head. "The thought never

crossed my mind. I'm just wondering if something in Atlanta—"

"Macon. I moved there about six weeks ago."

"Then did something or someone in Macon follow you here?"

"Negative, as they say in law enforcement."

He smiled, which relieved some of the tension.

"I haven't lived in Macon long," Hannah continued. "I've got a job working retail, a small apartment, and the only folks I know, other than a few people at church, are the ladies at work. Most of whom are in their fifties and early sixties. Not a guy wearing blue flannel in the bunch."

"And in Atlanta?"

She studied the passing countryside. "I lived there for three years and had a number of friends. Perhaps I stepped on a few toes, although I couldn't say for sure."

"Anyone give you a hard time?"

"Meaning what?"

Lucas tilted his head but kept his eyes on the road. "Maybe a guy who came on to you but who you didn't like. Someone who tried to get a bit too close. Anything like that?"

She turned her head, grateful for the wide brim of the bonnet that hid her face lest he read something from her expression. Brian Walker. He would fit Lucas's profile of a person to watch.

"You've turned quiet again," Lucas said.

"Just sorting through all the guys I knew and coming up empty-handed as far as your parameters. I'm sure Mr. Flannel is a local problem. I told you he was in the filling station when I turned off the highway. I'd never seen him before that moment."

"Yet he followed you."

"Because of my sister. The news video was playing on the television. The older man commented on my resemblance to the woman in the news clip."

"Do you and Miriam look alike?"

"Some say we do. I'm taller. Bigger boned. I take after my father."

"And Miriam?

"In looks, she's her mother's daughter." So very much so.

"Yet the old guy at the gas station saw enough of a resemblance to comment about it?"

"He was speculating and probably trying to drum up a little excitement. It was the middle of the night. I doubt much happens in this part of the country that's exciting."

Then she thought of what *had* happened— her mother had been killed and her two younger sisters kidnapped.

"Look, I'm rambling." She waved her hand in the air. "And not thinking straight. Forgive me. Let me assure you I haven't seen anyone in the area who reminds me of the folks I knew or had business dealings with in Atlanta. This guy in blue is a home-grown problem who wants information about Miriam for whatever reason."

He also wanted Hannah, which she wouldn't mention. Not when she was riding in a buggy in plain sight. Would Lucas be able to save her if the guy came after her again? That was a question Hannah didn't want to voice.

Lucas kept his eyes on the terrain around them, watching for anything that spelled danger. He flicked a quick glance into the rear of the buggy where he had stashed his rifle. Not that he wanted to use it, but some precautions were necessary, especially if he wanted to keep Hannah safe.

She hadn't spoken in longer than he would have liked, but he wouldn't interrupt her thoughts with idle chatter. A lot had happened recently that she needed to ponder. He hadn't told her about his former life as a cop and wondered if that would make a difference. At first, she had seemed hesitant to talk to Deputy Gainz when they had stopped at the sheriff's office in Willkommen yesterday. Some people struggled with law enforcement. He hoped that wasn't the case with Hannah.

Although having her mother murdered and her two sisters kidnapped was reason enough, especially when at least one of the men who had stopped Miriam's car had been law enforcement. A rotten apple could spoil the whole bushel, as folks who grew apples in this area of Georgia knew all too well.

Olivia. His hands tightened on the reins. She hadn't been dirty; she'd been set up. Lucas had tried to track down the culprits responsible. Someone had planted the marked bills in her apartment just as sure as two guys working for Vipera had killed her on that fateful night. The memory of finding her body sprawled on the dock struck him like a rock that tightened his gut and made him gasp.

Hannah turned to him. "Are you okay?"

"Sorry." He struggled to find his voice. "I must have been daydreaming."

"I'd call it more of a nightmare from the sound you made."

He fisted his right hand and tapped it against his chest. "Probably indigestion." He smiled, hoping she would buy his explanation. "Or too much coffee."

"Do you know the Glick family?"

"Fannie does. She said they're nice folks."

"What about the daughter?" Hannah asked.

"Amish children are seen and not heard, as the saying goes. Fannie knew who Rosie was, but I doubt she had any interaction with the girl."

"What about Belinda, who works at Fannie's store? Were she and Rosie friends?"

"A good question and one I can't answer. Fannie might know."

He flicked the reins and considered Hannah's question. The girl at the inn had given Hector the note that led to Hannah's confrontation with the attacker. Belinda had been seen talking to a man earlier in the day. Could both girls have been involved with men who were in some way tied in with the hijacking of Hannah's mother and sisters?

Lucas rubbed his right hand over his aching leg that often acted up in the cold. Not that he would complain. His injury had been minor compared to what Olivia had endured. Some days he wondered if he'd let her down since he'd left Savannah. His career in law enforcement had ended because he'd gotten too close to someone. Had it been Eugene Vipera?

His eyes left the road momentarily to stare at the mountain. Over the rise and on the other side was the Pine Lodge Mountain Resort, one of Vipera's many assets.

Lucas had traveled to the North Georgia mountains in the hope of uncovering dirt on the wealthy tycoon who he was convinced had played a role in Olivia's death. But the trail that had led him here had dried up and made him realize he was following a false lead. As far as he could determine, Vipera had never even visited the lodge and left the operation to a number of managers and a board of directors.

For the last eleven months, Lucas had pushed anything to do with law enforcement aside to let his body and his psyche heal. The wound to his pride had been harder to deal with than the gunshot he'd taken.

Fannie had provided a balm for both. Her motherly ways had brought him from the brink of darkness and allowed him to live again. The clear air and wholesome lifestyle had soothed his pain and made him realize there was more to life than crime and corruption.

Now he felt the pull back to his old ways and his former life. Mentally he drew a triangle between the two Amish girls and Vipera. Then he placed Hannah's sisters and her mother in the center and circled them with a bull's-eye before he glanced at Hannah.

If her family had been in the bull's-eye, she might be, as well.

"I've got a brother, but no sisters," Lucas

stated. Seeing her surprise made him realize his mistake.

"Sorry," he said, hoping to clear up her confusion. "I must have thought you could read my mind. Let me backtrack a bit. I don't know much about girls, but they like to share secrets, right?"

Hannah shrugged. "I guess they do, although I'm not a good person to ask."

"But you're a girl. You know how women think, even teenage women."

Her mouth tugged into a weak smile. "How very astute of you to realize that I'm a girl. The truth is I never had many friends growing up."

"Really?"

"We moved too often. My mother never stayed anyplace more than a few months. Children adjust, no matter the circumstances, so early in life I learned the folly of making friends only to leave those friends behind. Some would call it a protective mechanism. Maybe it was but, for whatever reason, I kept to myself."

"You and your sisters must have been close."

Hannah tugged at a strand of her hair that had escaped the bun and the bonnet.

Had she heard him? Before he repeated his question, she sighed. "Miriam and I were sisters. I wouldn't call us friends."

Lucas turned his gaze back to the road. "What about Sarah?"

Hannah's expression softened. "Sarah was different."

"Because she was the baby?"

"Maybe. I'm not sure. It probably sounds strange, but for the last few years—in fact, most of our teen years—Miriam and I seemed to be competing with each other. I never felt the need to prove myself when it came to Sarah."

"You and Miriam were closer in age?"

"Two years apart, which could have had bearing on our relationship. I don't know when the competition with Miriam started or why."

"Did your mother recognize the struggle between you two?"

"It's hard to say. She and Miriam were always close. I never felt like I fit in."

"Usually the oldest is the favorite. I'm the middle child and never felt that I measured up."

"I'm sorry, Lucas. It's not easy growing up without feeling secure."

"It may have helped me succeed."

"Meaning?"

"College, to get ahead in my job."

"You mean you haven't always worked at the inn?" Sarcasm was evident in her comment.

He'd said too much. "There was a time before the inn, but I'm happy here in the mountains."

"And the life you lived before?" she asked.

"It's over. Let's leave it at that."

Lucas was grateful she didn't press him for more information. Some things needed to remain in the past, back in Savannah, on that dock.

TEN

Lucas's comments added anxiety to Hannah's already unsettled day. She didn't like to discuss her past or her estranged relationship with Miriam. The pain of what she had learned the night she'd left her family in Knoxville remained an open wound she feared would never heal.

Her mother's caustic words still stung. Miriam and Sarah had returned home long after their mother had become enraged and hadn't realized what had transpired. Maybe that was a blessing.

Hot tears burned Hannah's eyes as she recalled her mother's accusation. "You're just like your father. He was a thief and so are you. I'm reporting you to the police."

"There's the turnoff to the Glick farm," Lucas said, interrupting her thoughts and bringing her back to the present.

She brushed her hand across her cheeks. Lucas, with his big heart and willingness to help, wouldn't understand her mother's assertion or the legacy that came with being her father's child.

Seemingly unaware of her upset, Lucas guided Daisy into the turn. The buggy jostled over the narrow dirt road. Holding on to steady herself, Hannah studied the farmland that stretched on each side of the roadway and the fallow fields waiting for spring planting. Surely Mr. Glick would be tending them soon.

The farmhouse appeared in the distance, a two-story, typical Amish structure in need of paint. Chickens plucked at the weeds in the side yard. A few head of cattle grazed on a distant pasture and a pair of horses stared at the buggy as it turned onto the gravel drive.

A barn, woodshed and outhouse sat at the rear of the main structure. A spindly tree, barren of leaves, grew near the house and would, undoubtedly, provide little shade in summer.

A child's face peered from the window. A little girl. Evidently Rosie Glick had a younger sister.

Lucas pulled up on the reins and turned to Hannah as the buggy stopped. "The Glicks have probably been inundated with police asking more questions than they would want to answer. They may have had their privacy interrupted by newsmen seeking a story, especially after your mother's death and your sisters' kidnappings were thought to be connected to their daughter's disappearance."

"You're saying we may not be welcome."

"I'm saying let's see what happens and go with the flow. I'll take the lead. You follow."

"You're sounding like a cop, and they happen to be my least favorite people."

His brow rose.

Again she'd said too much. "Nothing personal."

"Right. Sounds like you've had a problem with law enforcement in the past?"

She nodded. "Leaving rental properties when our mother couldn't pay the rent made our family cautious around anyone in uniform."

"Tough way to live as a kid," he said, climbing down from the buggy.

"Some folks have it worse."

He nodded. "You're right."

A cold wind blew from the mountain and made her shiver. She adjusted the cape and was grateful for Lucas's strong arms when he helped her down.

She glanced at the house.

Was anyone home? The child had disappeared. Or had she been a figment of Hannah's imagination?

The girl had reminded her of Sarah when she

was four years old and left alone too often when Miriam and Hannah were at school and their mother had to work. Hannah should have done more to protect her sister.

Now Sarah was gone.

Hannah's heart weighed heavy as she and Lucas climbed the steps to the front porch. He moved in front of her and knocked on the door.

He rapped again and then turned to study the fields and pastures. His gaze brightened. He tapped her arm and pointed. "Someone's coming from the field."

She turned to see a man dressed in the Amish waistcoat and black felt hat.

Lucas left the porch and met him in the drive. Hannah followed then stepped back a few feet, unsure if she would be welcomed. At least Lucas looked the part, whether he was true Amish or not.

Glancing down at the blue calf-length dress and black cape, she realized her mistake. She looked Amish, as well.

"Yah?" The farmer eyed Lucas and ignored Hannah. Perhaps women were to be seen and not heard, just like the children, as Lucas had mentioned.

He extended his hand. The farmer hesitated and then accepted the handshake.

"I'm Lucas Grant. I work for Fannie Stoltz at the Amish Inn. She sends her greetings."

"I do not know your face."

Lucas nodded as if understanding the farmer's confusion. "I have not lived long in the mountains. Fannie has given me a job and the community has accepted me, for which I am grateful."

"You are here for a reason?"

Hannah appreciated the Amish's way to cut to the chase. They didn't waste time on idle chitchat.

Lucas motioned Hannah forward. "I am here with Hannah Miller. Her mother was killed on the mountain two months ago. Her sisters were kidnapped. Perhaps you have heard of this?"

The farmer's expression never changed.

"There is speculation," Lucas continued, "that your daughter's disappearance could be tied to what happened to the Miller family."

Mr. Glick pursed his lips. "I have already talked to the police."

"Yes, sir. I'm sure you have, but the police will not share the information with us. You can understand Hannah's concern and her desire to learn more about what happened to her sisters."

Mr. Glick blinked but refused to respond.

"Could you tell us about the young man Rosie was seeing?"

The farmer's gaze darkened. "I do not need to talk about my daughter. Talking will not bring her back."

"Sir, she may have been involved with the same people who captured Hannah's sister. If so, the women may be together. The more we can learn about what happened to Rosie, the better able we'll be to find both of them."

"Rosie is gone." The father's voice was devoid of inflection.

"You probably think she left of her own volitions, of her own choice, but that might not be the case, sir. Rosie could have been kidnapped. If so, we need to find her."

The door to the house opened and a woman stepped onto the front porch. Her brown dress hung loose over her bony shoulders. Her face was drawn tight and a kerchief covered her head and tied under her chin.

"Tell them, Wayne. Rosie was a good girl. She would not leave without telling me where she was going."

The husband did not respond to his wife's plea.

"I told you of my dream," she pressed.

He stared at his wife. "We do not believe in dreams, Emma."

"And what of scripture? Has not *Gott* worked through dreams?"

"He does not work in that way today."

Hannah stepped forward, hearing the pain in the woman's voice. "Mrs. Glick, I believe in dreams."

A flicker of hope washed over the woman's face. "I saw her. I saw Rosie. She was crying for me to find her."

Hannah glanced at Mr. Glick. "Sir, if we can track the boyfriend, we might be able to find your daughter."

Glick's eyes narrowed. "The police have not found her."

"The police initially thought she had run off with Will MacIntosh," Hannah tried to explain. "I doubt they put much effort into the investigation."

"*Yah*, it is only when the *Englischer* women are attacked that they think about the needs of my daughter."

Mr. Glick's comment had merit.

Lucas stepped closer. "I don't know how the police operate here, but I do know that the sheriff has been in the hospital with a gunshot wound and the sheriff's office is staffed by an older deputy and a few new hires. The deputies may have tried their best, but their best might not be good enough."

"Tell them." Mrs. Glick moved toward her

husband and grabbed his arm. "Tell them about the man."

Mr. Glick swallowed as if the words were stuck in his throat. "Rosie was a good girl. One day I found her wearing a necklace of shiny beads. She did not think I had seen them, and she tried to tuck them into her dress. The boy had given them to her."

"Will MacIntosh?"

He nodded.

"Will lived on the county road not far from here. The police said she had run off with him. The neighbors said they had seen them together. He lived alone and worked at the lodge."

"What happened to him?"

"I went to his trailer. His things were still there, but he was gone. I found the beads he had given Rosie broken on the ground outside. They had hurried away and had not taken time to pack. He lived over the county line in Petersville. The police there did not think anything of them leaving. I told them Rosie was a good daughter who would not do such a thing, but they told me I was naive and did not realize how a teen would want something other than the Amish way."

"What about the sheriff in Willkommen?" Lucas asked.

"He was more interested, but he said it wasn't his jurisdiction."

Hannah had thought the father unfeeling at first, but she caught a glimpse of the pain he carried.

"I do not understand," Glick continued. "A sheriff who would not search for a girl no matter who was in charge of the investigation."

Lucas nodded. "Once the sheriff is released from rehab, I'll see what he has to say. Perhaps one of his deputies will talk to you again."

Mr. Glick shook his head. "I do not wish to talk to anyone."

He took his wife's arm. "Come, Emma. We must go inside."

"But, Wayne."

He motioned her forward. She glanced at Hannah, pain written on her face. Then, like a dutiful wife, she followed her husband up the steps. He entered the house. Mrs. Glick hesitated for a moment and then glanced at them over her shoulder.

"Find Rosie," she said, her voice almost a whisper. "Find my daughter."

Mr. Glick's reaction troubled Lucas. He had, no doubt, been questioned too many times already and saw no point in revealing facts about his daughter to anyone again. The pain both parents felt had to be heart-wrenching.

Mrs. Glick's desire to obey her husband, as was the Amish way, seemed to conflict with her heart that had to be broken.

"I wonder if Mrs. Glick knows more than she was willing to share," Lucas said as Daisy pulled the buggy onto the dirt road and headed toward the paved blacktop.

"Information her husband didn't want her to share." Hannah shook her head with regret. "Why are Amish men so insensitive to their wives' feelings?"

"It might seem that way, especially today, but remember Mr. Glick is trying to protect his daughter's reputation and his family's privacy. He's been interrogated by the Petersville police. Their tactics may have been cold and callous, and even more so, considering the circumstances. Then if he repeated everything to the Willkommen sheriff without any good coming from either branch of law enforcement, he may have lost trust in the *Englisch* ways."

Hannah nodded. "When you say it like that, I can almost see his point and take his side. Yet nothing can be done if we don't know more about the young man who showed an interest in their daughter."

"Deputy Gainz provided directions to the

county road, and Mr. Glick mentioned that MacIntosh lived in a trailer. When I first moved here, I took my buggy over most of this area to get to know the terrain, including the county road. I seem to recall seeing a few trailers."

He glanced at Hannah to make certain she would agree to his plan. "We could look for a mailbox that might bear the kid's last name. MacIntosh isn't common around these parts. Most surnames are either German or Amish. A Scottish name might stand out or be remembered by one of the neighbors."

"It's worth a try."

He nodded. "The county road isn't far."

In less time than Lucas had expected, the sign for the road appeared on the left. "The turnoff's less than two miles from the Glick farm," he noted. "An easy walk, especially for an Amish girl used to hoofing it around the county."

"Did I tell you that I don't like this guy, whoever he is?"

Lucas nodded in agreement. "I don't like anyone who preys on women."

A small clapboard house sat back from the road. Lucas slowed as they passed the mailbox. "Koenig means 'king' in German," Lucas said, referring to the name stenciled on the box.

"A far cry from MacIntosh."

Continuing on, they passed a number of houses without names on the mailboxes.

Lucas was starting to feel discouraged. "We'll go a bit farther and then turn around."

"There." Hannah pointed to the right. "Behind the white house. It looks like a trailer sits back from the main structure. Let's check the mailboxes and see if we can find a name."

Pulling Daisy to a stop, Lucas peered at the two mailboxes and felt a sense of relief when he spied *MacIntosh* written on one of the boxes with what appeared to be a wide-tipped Sharpie. Someone had painted over the marker with a thin coat of white paint that failed to completely cover the ink.

"I think we've found Mr. MacIntosh's home."

Lucas pulled onto the dirt drive and slowly headed past the small house. A muscular dog with Rottweiler markings barked from the front porch.

"So much for trying to go unnoticed," Lucas grumbled.

A hand-painted sign was nailed to a tree: Trailer for Rent. Lucas turned the buggy onto the narrow path that angled toward the trailer.

Hannah glanced back at the house. "I hope the homeowner doesn't think we're trespassing."

"We'll say we're interested in renting."

Lucas pulled Daisy to a stop in front of the trailer. "Might be safer if you stay in the buggy."

She shook her head. "I'm going with you." She climbed down and hurried to join him as he neared the door.

Again she flicked her gaze back at the clapboard house. "I'm worried, Lucas."

He understood her concern. "I didn't see a No Trespassing sign. Remember we're here in hopes of renting the trailer."

A cobweb stretched across the front door. "Doesn't look like anyone's been here for some time."

He wiped the web away and knocked on the door. Hearing no one inside, he grabbed the door handle, expecting it to be locked.

The door opened.

"People in the country often forget the importance of security." He held up his hand. "Wait here, Hannah."

She grabbed his arm. "I'm not leaving your sight."

She was frightened, at least somewhat.

"Isn't it against the law to break and enter a private property?" She rubbed her hands over her arms and glanced again over her shoulder.

"That's a question for law enforcement," he answered, once again thankful she didn't know about his past.

He climbed the few stairs into the trailer and was surrounded by stale air and more cobwebs. A roach scurried underfoot. "Watch out for critters."

"Meaning—"

"Meaning anything could have taken up residence here."

He glanced at the small table and bench seats. A magazine was tossed open to one side. Lucas flipped it over, noting the name on the mailing label. William MacIntosh.

"Let's see if we can find anything the police failed to uncover." Lucas glanced around the cramped space. "If they even did a search."

While Hannah peered into the bathroom, Lucas entered the bedroom. A blanket and top sheet were strewed across the thin mattress. He walked around the bed and leaned down. Using a tissue he pulled from a box on the small side table, he lifted a white ribbon from the floor.

"One of the ties on an Amish bonnet?" she asked from the hallway.

"Maybe." He folded the tissue around the ribbon and tucked it inside his shirt.

"Anything in the bathroom?"

Hannah shook her head. "Nothing I could find."

Lucas glanced at the commode, sink and shower before opening the kitchen drawers and cabinets. He rustled through the odds and ends, none of which provided clues to either William MacIntosh or his Amish girlfriend.

He opened the refrigerator. A half gallon of what must have been milk sat on the top shelf filled with a black rotting mass of bacteria. He checked the vegetable bin and freezer and then closed the door and turned aside to pull in a lungful of air.

Once they had searched the rest of the trailer, he motioned to Hannah. "Let's get going."

Pushing open the narrow front door, he blew out a stiff breath. His pulse raced and his gut tightened as he stared down the barrel of what appeared to be a Remington .308 rifle.

Leaving his own rifle in the buggy had been his first mistake. Placing Hannah in danger followed a close second.

"Hands in the air," the burly guy behind the rifle demanded. "Nice and slow. The rifle's loaded and, in case you didn't notice, my finger is on the trigger. Now step outside and don't try anything funny."

"I'm so sorry, sir." Hannah smiled sweetly as she followed Lucas out of the trailer, acting completely unfazed by the man or his weapon. "We are new to the area and need a place to live. I saw your sign about a trailer for rent." Her voice dripped with sincerity.

The tension in the man's neck seemed to ease. "Where're you folks from?"

"Tennessee," she answered with another warm smile. "We need lodging, but money is tight."

"I haven't cleaned up the place since the last tenant left."

Hannah batted her long lashes. The muscular guy appeared taken by her pleasant disposition and pretty face.

"If you don't mind—" Lucas pointed to the rifle. "We're not out to do any harm."

"Sorry." The landlord lowered the weapon. "I came home from work and saw the buggy."

"Our mistake," Lucas admitted. He glanced at Hannah. "As she mentioned, we are eager to find a place to live."

The guy sniffed and rubbed his jaw. "I could rent you the place starting this weekend. Soon as I get it cleaned up."

"How much would you charge per month?" Hannah asked.

The landlord quoted a figure that seemed steep, especially considering the condition of the trailer.

"The tenant must have left in a hurry," Hannah mused.

The big guy nodded. "Without paying his last month's rent."

"Any idea where he went?" She continued to press.

"No clue." The landlord looked at Lucas's wide-brimmed hat and Hannah's bonnet. "You folks Amish?"

Lucas hesitated then nodded.

"I saw an Amish girl here a few times," the guy continued. "Maybe I should have said something, but I figured it wasn't any of my business."

"How old was she?"

"Sixteen or seventeen."

Hannah glanced at Lucas. He nodded and then placed his hand on the small of her back. "If I can find work, we might be interested in renting your place."

He ushered her toward the buggy. "We'll be in touch."

"Just let me know." The landlord waved and then stepped into the trailer.

Lucas helped Hannah into the buggy and climbed in beside her. He flicked the reins, hurrying Daisy along the dirt road. They passed the white-clapboard house on the left. From the looks of the rotten soffits and peeling paint, the landlord didn't maintain his own home, either.

A dog barked.

"Look, Lucas." Hannah pointed to where the

Rottweiler foraged in the underbrush. He continued to bark as if trying to get their attention.

Lucas pulled Daisy to a stop. "Stay in the buggy."

Glancing at the trailer to make sure the landlord was still inside, Lucas approached the dog, who clawed at the loosened soil and whined. Either the dog or another animal had dug a hole and had unearthed something of interest.

Moving closer, Lucas peered down at a partially uncovered shoe. A work boot that appeared to be encasing a human bone.

The hair on Lucas's neck rose.

He turned to Hannah. "Did you bring your cell phone?"

She nodded and pulled it from under her cape. "Do you need to make a call?"

"I want to take a photo of what the dog found."

She accessed the camera app and handed him the cell.

Working quickly, he snapped a series of shots and then climbed back in the buggy.

"Call Deputy Gainz." Lucas provided the number for the sheriff's office. Once they turned onto the main road, she tapped in the number and handed him the phone.

"We stopped at Will MacIntosh's trailer and found a ribbon that may be from an Amish bonnet," Lucas told the deputy once he was on the line. "A thorough search by your crime-scene folks might turn up additional evidence, but that's not the main reason I'm calling."

"Did something happen?" the deputy asked.

"The landlord has a dog. Looks like a mix of Rottweiler and some other big breed. He burrowed in the dirt and uncovered a work boot and what appears to be a human fibula."

Lucas glanced at Hannah, who was staring at him wide-eyed.

"I'll send you pictures, but you need to check it out yourself, Deputy. I'm ninety-nine-percent certain the bone isn't from a farm animal."

"What are you saying?"

"I'm saying someone killed Will MacIntosh and either dumped his body or buried it in a shallow grave directly across the path from the landlord's house."

"What about Rosie?"

"My guess is that she was kidnapped, held captive and maybe trafficked."

Lucas glanced at Hannah before he shoved the cell closer to his ear. "Or she might be dead."

Hannah could only hear one side of his conversation with the deputy, but Lucas's words chilled her. What if Rosie had been killed and buried along with her boyfriend?

An even more chilling thought played through her mind. She gasped, tears filled her eyes and she grabbed for the seat, needing something to hold on to as her world spun out of control. Only, instead of the seat, she found Lucas's hand.

"Take a deep breath." His voice was filled with concern. "Clear your mind of whatever you're thinking because I'm more than positive that they'll find the boyfriend's remains in the grave, but not Rosie's, and not your sister's, either."

She nodded and tried to do as he suggested, but she kept seeing Sarah's big eyes filled with tears the night she'd left home.

"I abandoned her." Tears streamed down Hannah's cheeks. "She thought I didn't love her and didn't care about her. Now I'm not even sure she's alive."

Hannah pulled her hand out of Lucas's grasp, wrapped her arms around her waist and bent over, unable to control her emotions.

He tugged on the reins and guided Daisy to a stop. Before she realized what had happened, his arms were around her, pulling her into his embrace. She nestled her head against his shoulder, feeling his strength and support.

The tears flowed. She cried for what had happened that night, for the terrible misunderstanding she'd had with her mother and for her unwillingness to explain the truth to Sarah. Hannah had chosen not to sully her youngest sister's relationship with their mother. In her heart, Hannah knew it had been the right thing to do, yet since then everything had turned out wrong.

"Shh," he said, his tone warm and soothing. Lucas's hand rubbed her shoulders. He rocked her like he would a child. The back-and-forth rhythm calmed her and filled her with a sense of acceptance.

"If anything happens to Sarah, I'll never forgive myself," she said, her voice raspy.

"You're not to blame for what happened."

As comforting as his words were, Lucas didn't know the truth about her past. "I left home. I left Sarah. She didn't understand."

"It was a decision you needed to make for your own well-being, Hannah. What happened on the mountain road has nothing to do with you leaving home."

"If I had remained in Tennessee, I could have insisted they stay put and not travel to Georgia."

"Are you sure? You might have agreed to the trip, as well. You could have been in the car the night it was stopped."

She shook her head. "You're wrong, Lucas."

"What could have happened isn't important,

Hannah. What matters is that you stay strong. You're not at fault. Two men captured your sisters. Miriam was able to escape. Sarah is still being held, but we'll find her."

"No one has found Rosie Glick."

"Because law enforcement mistakenly thought she had run off with her boyfriend."

"She could be dead."

"She could also be alive," Lucas countered. "If this group is trafficking women, they want to keep the girls alive. That's a good thing. We just need to find them."

"There's nothing to go on."

"Not yet, but something will break now that law enforcement realizes that the two disappearances may be connected. If we find Rosie, we might find Sarah, as well."

Hannah closed her eyes for a long moment and willed her mind to clear. She couldn't think of what might be. Just as Lucas had said, she had to remain optimistic and focused on the present.

Easier said than done.

"Let's go back to the inn." He squeezed her shoulder and relaxed his hold as she pulled out of his grasp. "You'll be safer there."

For all her life, Hannah had never known anyone who was totally focused on her welfare.

Not until she had met Lucas. She felt secure with him.

But she had also felt secure with Brian. Then she'd done some investigating on her own and had found out the truth about him that was both painful and humiliating. She'd been such a fool.

Maybe God was giving her a second chance, although Lucas was hesitant to talk about his past. Maybe he was hiding from something, as well. Perhaps they were alike in that way. She wouldn't give voice to her mistakes, and she was afraid to ask him to reveal the truth about his own.

She couldn't take any more disappointment. Not today after she'd found comfort in his arms. Hannah would rather live in the moment.

If only she could.

ELEVEN

Hannah was heavyhearted when they returned to the inn. The fresh air had been invigorating and she enjoyed the side-to-side rhythm of the buggy over the roadway and the sound of the horse's hooves clip-clopping on the pavement, but she kept thinking of the two young women gone missing.

Lucas pulled to a stop in front of the Amish Store, where the mechanic was standing.

"How'd the wheel work?" Calvin asked, glancing at the back of the buggy.

"No problems. You did a good job."

"You've got a good horse and a good driver. That makes a difference." He glanced at Hannah and tipped his head. "Afternoon, ma'am."

She smiled in return but didn't speak, wondering if the kindly gentleman recognized her. He wasn't saying and she wouldn't ask.

"We've got a new guest," the mechanic said.

"Oh?"

Hannah's pulse quickened fearing who might have moved into the B and B.

"You know Sheriff Kurtz? He was getting rehab in the Willkommen nursing home, but they released him today. Fannie said he's not strong enough to be on his own, so she insisted he come here for a week or two."

"Fannie's a good woman," Lucas said as he flicked his gaze to the inn. "I need to talk to the sheriff. What room's he in?"

"Room three," Calvin replied. "The room on the corner."

Where Hannah had stayed.

She stole another glance at Calvin, but his attention was once again focused on the wheel he had fixed. Perhaps she need not worry about anyone at the inn questioning her identity.

The horse obeyed the flick of Lucas's wrist and headed across the property and back to the barn located near the Amish homes.

Hannah kept her head down lest they pass anyone, still concerned she might be recognized. She didn't want questioning eyes on her, especially after the young woman had passed the note to Hector yesterday.

"What about Belinda?" she asked.

Lucas leaned closer. "I'll talk to her when she comes back to work tomorrow."

"Are you sure people won't recognize me?"

"I don't think you need to worry, Hannah."

Easy enough for him to say. But she was worried. Even more so after stopping by Will MacIntosh's trailer.

"Lucas, are you sure the bone you saw was human?"

He hesitated before responding. "I know it upset you, but MacIntosh probably got too cocky or maybe he no longer wanted to be involved in whatever was happening. He might have attempted to shove his weight around. Somebody wanted to teach him a lesson."

"The lesson went too far." Hannah shivered not from the cold but from the thought of a man being murdered.

The road turned and in the distance the two Amish homes were visible. Fannie's house looked warm and inviting set against the mountain range in the distance and the low foothills.

Cattle grazed in the pasture and two deer nibbled on bushes at the far end of the landscaped area that surrounded the inn. Hannah glanced at the tall windows in the dining room, seeing the twinkling lights. Was the sheriff there, enjoying a meal? If so, would he want information about her past and perhaps do his own investigation? What would Fannie and Lucas think of her if they found out about her father?

She clutched her hands together and bit down

on her lip, trying to stem the worry that bubbled up within her. How foolish to think she could hide the truth from anyone.

"Coming here was a mistake," she said aloud even before she realized the words had escaped her mouth.

"You're tired and worried. Probably hungry and cold, too. You'll feel better once we get to Fannie's house."

"I'm not sure, Lucas. If it weren't for me, the guy in flannel wouldn't be hanging around. He's after me for whatever reason and he's putting everyone else in danger. That's my fault."

"No one is accusing you, Hannah."

"Thank you for that, but I know the peace and quiet of this mountain inn has changed. I'm worried about innocent people who might get hurt."

"So far the guy hasn't harmed anyone except you."

"And Simon."

Lucas nodded. "You're right. Simon was injured, but I blame it on the man who attacked him. He's the one who's stirring up trouble, not you. You're here to find your sisters."

"What were they doing on the mountain?" She dropped her head into her hand and sighed. "I can't understand why they traveled to Willkommen."

"The deputy mentioned that they wanted to find your mother's estranged sister, but maybe the sheriff will have more information."

She lifted her head, feeling a swell of encouragement. "Do you think so?"

"We can talk to him if he feels like having visitors. He was involved in the investigation of your mother's death. He's bound to know more than the deputy."

"But he probably won't divulge Miriam's whereabouts."

"He'll know if she's safe and that's the most important thing, right? If she's with Abram Zook as people have mentioned, then you probably don't have to worry. He'll take care of her."

Lucas pulled the mare to a stop at the back door of Fannie's house. He climbed to the ground and helped Hannah down, his hands holding her tight and secure.

"Thank you," she said as her feet touched the ground.

His hands remained around her waist for a long moment. He stared down at her, question in his gaze. Behind him, the rays of the sun bathed both of them in an ethereal glow that seemed surreal.

Being in Lucas's arms was so unlike anything she had experienced before. She didn't want to move lest he drop his hands and step away from her.

She lifted her face expectantly. He lowered his lips to hers and time stood still. Everything that had happened in her life—all the darkness and pain—faded away. For one sweet instant, she was totally enveloped in goodness and hope and light.

The kitchen door opened. Hannah's heart plummeted.

"There you are." Fannie stepped onto the porch. "I was beginning to wonder if you would ever return."

A sense of loss filled Hannah as Lucas moved back and grabbed the reins. "We ran into a bit of a problem."

"Oh, no."

"Hannah can tell you about it while I unharness the mare and get her settled in the barn."

Only Hannah didn't know if she could talk about anything, except how much she wanted to return to Lucas's arms.

"Tell me, dear, all about what happened." Fannie motioned her inside. "I have water on the stove if you'd like a cup of tea."

With a nod, Hannah pulled in a fortifying breath. She needed to focus on the present instead of a handsome man who made her dream of what could be.

"Tea sounds perfect," she told Fannie. Hopefully the warm beverage would calm her racing pulse and make her forget how much she had wanted Lucas to kiss her again.

After hanging the cape and bonnet on a peg just inside the kitchen, she helped Fannie fix a pot of tea and then recounted what they had found as she sipped a cup of the inviting brew.

"Will the coroner be able to tell if the remains are from the young man?" Fannie asked after Hannah had shared what had happened.

"I believe the medical examiner or even the Georgia Bureau of Investigation will get involved," Lucas said as he entered the kitchen and overheard Fannie's comment. "The forensic folks will be better able to make an identification."

"That poor young man," Fannie said.

"He was probably involved in illegal activity, Fannie. Hopefully we'll find out more about him once the results come back from the GBI."

"The tea's hot," Fannie told him. "There's coffee, as well."

Lucas poured a cup of coffee and nodded his gratitude as he took a long swig. His gaze met Hannah's, and the memory of his kiss made her face flush.

"The temperature's dropping," he said. Then he glanced away as if not realizing what that kiss had meant to her. "I thought we could expect warmer weather, but you can't fool with Mother Nature."

"Spring will be here soon enough," Fannie assured him. "New buds are on the Bradford pear trees."

"They're always so beautiful," Hannah said wistfully, recalling the flowering trees in Knoxville that dotted the landscape. "I'm sure spring is lovely here at the inn."

A heaviness tugged at her heart. She wouldn't stay long enough to see the trees and flowers bloom. She would be in Macon or in some other small town, trying to make a life for herself.

"Did you talk to the sheriff?" Lucas asked Fannie.

"*Yah.* He does not want to be coddled, but he is not as strong as he thinks. The man can be stubborn." Fannie smiled impishly. "He will hurt himself if he pushes too hard. I told him he could not do any work for the first week he is here. He did not like that, but it was the only way I would agree to having him stay with us."

"You and the sheriff are friends?" Hannah asked.

Fannie smiled knowingly. "Yes, for many years. He was new to Willkommen when we first met. My father did not think he was someone with whom I should spend time."

There was a longing in Fannie's voice that Hannah had not heard before. Then just that quickly, the Amish woman wiped her hands on a napkin and rose. "You have reminded me that I must check on him." She glanced at Hannah. "Lucas has chores, but you can join me. I think you want to talk to him about your sisters. You could also tell him what you found today."

"I'm…" She glanced at Lucas.

His gaze softened. "You don't have to be fearful of the sheriff."

"Of course not. I'm not afraid. It's just that—"

She didn't want either of them to learn the truth about her past and about the man who had given her life. Her gut tightened. She rubbed her hand over her abdomen, hoping to stem the rumble that ensued.

"You are tired and would perhaps want to rest?" Fannie offered.

"Yes, that's it exactly. I just need to shut my eyes for a few minutes."

Hannah pushed away from the table, carried the cup to the sink and left it on the sideboard, and then hurried upstairs to get away from both their questioning gazes. Hannah needed time to forget Lucas's kiss and gather strength and the wherewithal to face the sheriff.

She didn't like law enforcement, never had, and especially not since her mother had threatened to call the authorities. Hannah needed to run away and pretend she had never been involved with her mother or her criminal dad.

Lucas was worried about Hannah. Today had almost been her undoing. He and Fannie left her to rest, locked the doors to the house and hurried to the inn. Fannie scurried into the kitchen to help with preparations for the evening meal while Lucas knocked at the sheriff's door.

"Sheriff Kurtz, it's Lucas Grant. If you're not too tired, I'd like to talk to you."

The door opened and the sheriff, looking a bit older and more stooped than he had the last time they had met, extended his hand. "Good to see you, Lucas. Come in. Fannie said you've been involved in a new situation."

Lucas closed the door and gave the sheriff time to return to the easy chair in the corner by the bed. "Draw up that other chair," the older man said, pointing to a straight-back chair near the door. "I never knew recuperation from a gunshot wound could take so long. Guess it says a lot for my age."

"Sir, from what I heard, you took a close-range hit to the abdomen. The surgeons had a lot of work to do."

"I'm not faulting their ability, mind you. I just don't appreciate being laid up so long. I expected to be back at my job by now, but the docs insist I need more time to heal."

Gingerly he rubbed his side. "I have to tell you they're right. No way I could sit at a desk or drive around in my squad car the way I'm feeling. Fannie invited me to stay at the inn. She claims three good meals a day and fresh air will have me back on my feet in no time."

"She's a thoughtful woman, and I know she's been worried about you. We all have."

"Appreciate it, Lucas. Coming close to death as the docs said I did makes a man look at life anew, if you know what I mean."

Lucas thought of his own gunshot wound. The ache in his leg was minor compared to what the sheriff had experienced. Still, Lucas could relate. His own inability to regain his strength had been a proverbial thorn in his flesh.

"You know, Fannie took me in when I was struggling," Lucas shared. "She gave me a dose of tough love when I started feeling sorry for myself. That coupled with her chicken soup got me on the right track. You'll be feeling strong in no time."

"Just so I don't get used to the soft life."

Lucas smiled. "I don't know if I've ever heard the Amish life called 'soft.'"

The sheriff laughed heartily and then so-bered. "You may have heard my story. I was raised Amish in Ethridge, Tennessee, but decided to leave the faith and moved to Georgia."

The sheriff's words took Lucas by surprise. "I'm doing just the opposite. After working here for the last eleven months and with Fannie's love for *Gott*, as she says, rubbing off on me, I'm considering seeking baptism."

"Have you talked to the bishop?"

Lucas shook his head. "Not recently. We talked a while back."

"From the sound of your voice, I take it the talk didn't go well."

Lucas shrugged. "He asked some direct questions and I answered truthfully. Seems I have a few issues to resolve before he can accept me as a member of his community."

The sheriff narrowed his eyes. "You told me you were a cop. That's not the easiest life, as we both know. Most folks thought I was crazy growing up Amish and then going into law enforcement."

"The two don't seem to coincide, do they, sir?"

"Not a bit. But there was something inside me that wanted to help. To make order out of some of the disorder I saw around me. I wanted that peaceful life for the folks I knew. No better way, in my opinion, than to be an officer of the peace."

Lucas appreciated the sheriff's take on law enforcement. Too many people thought cops went into criminal justice to carry a gun and order people around, which was the farthest thing from the truth.

"I appreciated you coming to me when you first arrived in this area, Lucas, and telling me about Savannah and the trouble you had experienced there. I told you then that I was sorry about your partner's death and knew you carried a heavy burden." The older man leaned closer. "You weren't at fault—I'm sure of that."

"She called me with information she'd received from a dubious source who I thought was taking her for a ride. We hadn't been able to find anything in two months. I doubted the new intel was legit."

"But she went in without you."

Lucas nodded. "She told me she wouldn't. Then the next thing I get a phone call telling me she's in trouble. I got there too late."

The sheriff steepled his fingers. "We all make mistakes, Lucas, although the mistake was your partner's and not yours. She should have waited for backup. But then, that's easy to say all these months later. I'm sorry for your loss."

Lucas nodded. "Thank you, sir. I thought I was over it. Then…" He hesitated. "Then I stumbled upon Hannah Miller in the woods."

Lucas told the sheriff what had happened and explained about the subsequent attacks and what they had found at Rosie Glick's boyfriend's trailer. "The two cases seem connected."

The sheriff rubbed his jaw. "You know we thought Rosie had run off. Hate to think we got that wrong and that she's been held captive all this time, especially if she's been caught in a trafficking operation."

"Did you talk to Miriam Miller? Hannah's worried about her whereabouts."

"She's safe. I've got an address to contact her somewhere in my things. As soon as I find it, I'll pass it on. Assure Hannah that her sister's with Abram Zook and he'll take care of her."

"I'll tell Hannah. What about Sarah? Supposedly she was carted off by a red-haired man."

"Which is what Miriam told us. I've had people looking for him. So far he hasn't surfaced." The sheriff shook his head with regret and then raised his gaze to Lucas. "What did you uncover in the Savannah operation?"

"A shipping tycoon by the name of Vipera. It's thought that he buys young, good-looking women and ships them out of the country on his cargo ships."

"Takes them to foreign countries?"

"Some, and some are taken to his private island where he entertains business people and government types from foreign countries."

"He needs to be stopped," the sheriff said.

"My thoughts exactly, but then someone wanted me out of the picture in Savannah. My partner was set up and they tried to get me, as well. I was politely told to turn in my badge and leave town."

"Seems the tycoon has pull, even with law enforcement."

"That's how I saw it. I had been wounded in a run-in with some of Vipera's goons and knew there was nothing I could do to change my past. I had to make a new future."

Again the sheriff stared long and hard at Lucas. "I think I know what caused the bishop to question whether you should join the Amish faith. He doesn't understand a man's need to bring the guilty to justice. Sometimes there's a fine line between justice and vindication."

Lucas didn't respond but he was relieved to know the sheriff understood. Lucas wanted to apprehend the thug who'd killed his partner even if retribution wasn't the Amish way. He also wanted to nab Vipera.

As much as he wanted to join the Amish faith, Lucas knew he'd be hard-pressed to turn the other cheek even if that was what the bishop demanded before he could gain entrance into the faith.

The sheriff narrowed his gaze. "Now tell me about this man who came after Hannah."

Lucas provided a description and recounted everything that had happened, which brought him back to today. "Rosie Glick's boyfriend worked at the lodge. Have you heard anything about that place?"

"Funny you should mention it. One of my deputies was in a vehicle accident the day Miriam escaped from her captor. He's been on a ventilator since then and hasn't been able to talk. According to his wife, he suspected something was going on at the lodge. High rollers from Atlanta and points south come in for a little hunting and fishing. My deputy suspected other things were happening, as well. The men rarely brought their wives and families, so I'll let you put the pieces together."

"Did he find proof of his suspicions?"

"Not that I know of, but his car was struck by a delivery van. The only info I have is that a small snake was on the side of the truck's paneling."

Lucas leaned forward in the chair, his pulse kicking up a notch. "Are you sure about the snake?"

"Deputy Garner spelled out a message, and I

determined he was trying to say 'snake.' Could have been wrong. I'm not sure. Why?"

"It's a long shot, sir, but as I mentioned, the shipping tycoon's last name is Vipera, which is a genus of venomous snakes. A coiled snake is part of his shipping logo. In fact, the night my partner was shot, she texted me, saying she had seen the snake."

"The tycoon?"

"Actually, two of his men. Vipera has a vast wealth and lots of holdings, including the Pine Lodge Mountain Resort. That's what drew me to this area initially. I was trying to find anything that might have bearing on my partner's death, but the trail went cold soon after I got here. In my search for evidence, I left no stone unturned but could find nothing that implicated Vipera in anything illegal on this end. The lodge is run by a group of managers, and Vipera has no involvement in the day-to-day operation."

The sheriff pursed his lips. "Yet if women have been taken around here and if the same thing has happened in Savannah, then there could be a very real trafficking connection."

Lucas nodded. "Which might be the link I was looking for."

"The problem is that I'm short-staffed, Lucas, or I'd send someone in to check out the lodge."

"The resort has been closed for renovation and is scheduled to open this weekend. Fannie delivers there. Pies, fresh-baked bread, produce. They placed an order for tomorrow. I'll make a delivery and check out what's going on."

"Everything will be under wraps, Lucas. I doubt they'll show any dirty laundry. They wouldn't be foolish enough to expose themselves."

"Sometimes the laundry is on the line and in full view, especially in an Amish area." He rose and extended his hand. "Thanks for giving me this time to talk, Sheriff."

The sheriff struggled to stand. "Wait a minute." He walked to a small suitcase beside his bed, unzipped the case and dug inside. "I know you're living Amish, but if you place yourself in danger, you'll need protection."

The sheriff pulled out a Glock, along with a holster and an extra magazine. "You might need this."

Lucas shook his head. "I left all that in Savannah. The only weapon I have is a .30-30 for hunting deer in season. I took it with me today because of Hannah but—"

"I understand, and that's commendable, yet you need to be realistic." Sheriff Kurtz held out the weapon. "Take it or I won't give you permission to help with this investigation."

"I'm not involved with the investigation, Sheriff. I'm trying to find two women who have disappeared."

"Then take it for the women."

Lucas thought of the firestorm he had walked into in Savannah. He hadn't expected the shooter. He hadn't expected being injured. He hadn't expected the surgery and recuperation. Then he thought of Olivia, who hadn't had backup and who had been slaughtered on a dock in the dead of night.

He raised his gaze to the sheriff, whose open expression told Lucas that he understood the former cop's conflict. "Thanks, sir." Lucas accepted the firearm. "I'll take the Glock, but I pray I won't have to use it."

"Stay safe," the sheriff cautioned.

Lucas nodded then hurried from the room, closing the door behind him.

The gun was heavy in his hand. He hadn't handled a sidearm in eleven months. He used to live with one, but he'd changed.

Night had fallen by the time he left the inn and hurried along the path, eventually seeing Fannie's house in the distance. A light appeared in the window. Hannah was waiting for him there.

She didn't know he was an ex-cop. The sheriff and Fannie were the only ones who knew.

Lucas couldn't be law enforcement and Amish. He couldn't carry a gun and be Amish. He couldn't embrace the *plain* way and be baptized into the faith and track down a killer.

But a killer was on the loose and he could have ties to the man who was coming after Hannah.

Amish or cop?

Lucas didn't know which he wanted to be.

"Hannah?" He unlocked the door and walked into the house calling her name. Only silence.

He turned and hurried back to the inn. Something didn't feel right in his gut.

Hannah? He started to run.

TWELVE

"I'm glad you had a nice nap and then came to help me with the sheriff's dinner," Fannie said as she carried the meal tray and walked next to Hannah. The two women headed along the hallway to room three, the room where Hannah had stayed two nights ago.

"I wonder if the sheriff has a minute to talk to me about my sisters." Hannah kept her voice low so as to not disturb the other guests.

"We can ask him, dear. Samuel is a very considerate man, although I know he might be tired after leaving rehab."

Before entering the far wing, Fannie stopped in her tracks and sighed. "Silly me. I forgot to bring his coffee." She turned and placed the tray in Hannah's hands. "Take this to Samuel while the food is still hot. I'll get the coffee from the kitchen."

Before Hannah could offer to run the errand,

Fannie was halfway down the hall, heading toward the dining area.

Hannah walked quickly to room three, stopped at the door and knocked lightly. "Sheriff? I have your dinner tray."

She heard a muffled response. Believing he had invited her to enter, she pushed open the door, stepped into the room and gasped.

A man stood over the sheriff. One hand was around his throat and the other was fisted as if to strike a blow.

"No!" Hannah screamed.

The man shoved past her, knocking the tray out of her hands. "Get outta my way."

She fell back against the doorjamb. The tray and its contents clattered onto the floor, the china plate shattering into tiny shards of porcelain.

Hannah struggled to her feet and stumbled toward the easy chair next to the bed where the older gentleman sat slumped, his head on his chest.

She touched his shoulder, fearing the worst.

A sound at the door made her turn. Was the assailant coming back to do more harm?

"Hannah?"

"Lucas, help me. The sheriff's been hurt."

Lucas was beside her, searching for the sheriff's pulse. "He's got a heartbeat. Come on, Sheriff. We need you to come to."

"It happened so fast," Hannah told him.

"Did you see the attacker?" Lucas asked.

She nodded, trying to find her voice.

"Who was it?"

"Oh, Lucas…" She gasped. "It was the same man who came after me. The man in the blue flannel shirt."

Lucas hadn't done enough, and Hannah had been placed in danger again. Thankfully the sheriff regained consciousness and seemed to be all right in spite of a blow to his jaw.

"The guy didn't expect me to fight back—that was evident," the sheriff said as he held an ice pack to his face. "He came up behind me and called me Hannah."

He looked at Fannie, sitting close by holding ice against her elbow. The assailant pushed her to the floor as he ran down the hallway and out the door.

"He kept saying 'Where is she?'" Fannie shared.

Lucas turned to look at Hannah, her hand resting on the older woman's shoulder.

"It's my fault," Hannah moaned. "He was looking for me. This is the room I stayed in the first night at the inn. The Hispanic man had delivered the note and the young Amish girl was involved. Belinda must have told him where I was staying." She looked down at Fannie. "The keys were hanging in the entryway."

"We changed that after you were attacked. Now the staff has to come to me to get a key."

"But he got in here somehow."

Lucas went to the bathroom and saw the open window. "He climbed in through here. The screen's been removed."

"That's my fault," the sheriff admitted. "The rehab facility was so warm. I always sleep better in a cold room. I opened the window to enjoy the fresh county air."

Lucas pointed to the wall. "From now on regulate the heat with the thermostat and keep the windows shut and locked. The open window was an invitation to him. With the curtains drawn and the lights out, he probably thought he could surprise Hannah if she was in the room or wait until she returned."

Although still shaken, Fannie excused herself and hurried to the kitchen to help with the evening meal. Deputy Gainz arrived soon after the sheriff notified him of the attack, and he and Lucas walked outside to survey the exterior of the inn.

"Removing the screen wouldn't have been difficult," Lucas admitted after they found the screen discarded in the bushes. "The open window allowed an easy entry, although the sill is about eight feet off the ground."

Gainz pointed to something in the underbrush.

Lucas neared and bent low. Two wooden boxes had been shoved under the bushes.

"My guess is the guy piled the boxes one atop the other," the deputy said. "That would give him enough leverage to hoist himself into the bathroom."

"Check the boxes for prints?"

"That's a good idea. If he's ever been arrested, we'll have him on file." Gainz glanced at the driveway and main entrance to the property. "Any idea where he could have parked his car?"

"He drives an SUV," Lucas reminded the deputy. "There's a back road that runs along the rear of the property. Easy enough to cut through the woods to get to his car and then head into Willkommen."

"Did you hear a vehicle leave the area?"

"No." Lucas shook his head. "But at the time, I wasn't listening for a car. I was trying to make sure the sheriff was all right."

"We've got a BOLO out for a dark Tahoe, although the guy could have more than one vehicle. I'm just glad the sheriff is okay. We're ready to have him back at his desk. I didn't sign on to be the head of the sheriff's department. Samuel was elected. Folks trust him. They know he'll do his best to keep them safe."

"You're doing a good job, Deputy Gainz."

He shook his head and laughed. "I can warm the seat of his chair, but that's about all. Ned Quigley's the expert. He's young and smart. He's got the ability and desire to run the sheriff's office, but he's at GBI headquarters, which I believe I mentioned when you stopped by the office. I had hoped Ned would be back by now."

"Does he know what happened?"

The deputy shook his head. "He's got enough on his plate without me calling and talking about our problems here."

"You might want to contact him in case he has the choice to stay or come back to Willkommen."

"I'll do that in the morning."

Lucas wondered if the deputy was truly interested in the new, younger deputy being called in. From what Lucas had been told, Gainz had worked for the town as long as most folks could remember. Sometimes a newcomer was hard to accept.

"We'll lock down the inn tonight and rig up some type of security on the main door," the deputy shared. "Everyone will have to go through the front entrance. It might be inconvenient for the staff, but we'll know who's coming and going. I don't want anyone else injured."

Especially not Hannah.

"You're certain Miriam is safe?" Hannah asked the sheriff as Lucas and the deputy returned to the guest bedroom.

"About as certain as I can be," Samuel said with a nod. "Abram won't let anything happen to your sister."

"And he's a good man?"

The sheriff smiled. "I've known him all his life, Hannah. Abram will protect your sister."

"You've known him all his life?" She repeated his comment, her brow furrowed. "I don't understand."

"Abram's my nephew."

"You're Amish?"

The sheriff laughed and shook his head. "No, but I grew up Amish. Ethridge, Tennessee, was my home."

Hannah glanced at Lucas. He saw the question in her eyes.

"If Abram needed a safe place to hole up," she said to Samuel, "would that safe place be Ethridge?"

The expression on the sheriff's face was enough to make Lucas realize that Hannah may have uncovered Miriam's whereabouts.

"Ethridge would be a safe destination," the sheriff acknowledged with a knowing smile. "If someone needed a place to hole up. I'll rummage through my things and try to find that address just as soon as my head clears a bit more."

Lucas's heart melted at the relief he read on Hannah's face. He glanced at the deputy, who was studying the window in the bathroom and hadn't heard the discussion. Just as well. Although the deputy was trustworthy, the fewer people who knew how to find Miriam, the better.

"What about Sarah?" Hannah asked.

The sheriff shook his head. "The new deputy who took over while I was having my surgery did everything he could to find her."

"He's the guy at the GBI now?" Lucas asked.

The sheriff nodded. "That's right. Ned Quigley. He briefed me on what he had found before he left for Atlanta. I'm sorry to say nothing has materialized on Sarah." The sheriff's eyes were heavy with regret. "No one has information about a red-haired man and no one has seen your sister."

"Did Quigley have a picture of her?"

The sheriff nodded. "One of the guys involved in the carjacking had pictures of both women on his smartphone."

"He also had a picture of Miriam?" Lucas asked.

The sheriff nodded again. "It appeared their

hands were bound. The women were seated on a chair, their hair was disheveled and they looked upset."

"Had the criminal sent the photos to someone else?" Lucas asked.

"All text and email messages had been deleted from the phone. Quigley took the mobile device to GBI headquarters. Their tech folks will try to uncover any contacts that might have left a cyber trail."

"Could you contact Quigley and check on the GBI's progress?"

The sheriff stared at Lucas for a long moment and then nodded, no doubt making the connection. "You're hoping they might find a trail that incriminates the shipping magnate in Savannah?"

"That would make everything fit together, don't you think?"

The sheriff nodded. "You never know what the GBI might be able to find."

"I don't understand," Hannah said.

Although Lucas didn't want to go into his past, Hannah needed to know. "I lived in Savannah. A shipping company there was thought to be involved in trafficking. I told the sheriff that it would be a huge coincidence, but the two operations might be connected."

"Although Georgia's not that big of a state," Samuel mused.

"Still," Hannah said, "it does seem unlikely."

"Let me know if you find out anything," Lucas said to the sheriff.

"I'll post a guard tonight." Gainz stepped back into the room.

Samuel groaned. "Do we have anyone to spare?"

The deputy jabbed a thumb at his chest. "You've got me. I may be getting close to retirement, but I can still pull surveillance and keep guard."

"Do you need help?" Lucas asked. "I can take a shift."

Gainz nodded. "I'll cover the first two hours. If you want to spell me at midnight, I'll catch a few winks then come back on at two a.m. Knowing the Amish, I'm sure some of your folks will be up by four. I'll wake you close to that time. That will get us through the night."

"I don't need a babysitter," the sheriff complained.

"No, sir, but there are other folks to think of at the inn."

"Of course there are." Samuel nodded. "I'm not thinking rationally."

He wiped his hand over his eyes.

"You're tired and need to rest." Lucas stood.

"The kitchen chores should be done and Fannie will probably be ready to return to her house. I'll walk her home." He glanced at Hannah. "Are you ready?"

She nodded. "What about you, Sheriff? Are you feeling okay?"

"After everything I've been through, a little scuffle and a jab to my chin isn't going to do any significant damage. You go on. We can talk tomorrow."

"How's Samuel?" Fannie asked when Hannah and Lucas entered the kitchen.

"He seems to be all right," Hannah assured her. "Although he'll probably have a sore jaw in the morning. I…I'm still so sorry."

Fannie patted Hannah's shoulder. "Stop thinking that way. You're not to blame. Is that clear?"

Fannie's stern gaze softened. "The sheriff has had worse happen to him. If he survived a gunshot to the stomach, he can survive a blow to his chin."

"Still—"

"No *stills* allowed, my little cabbage."

Hannah laughed at the older woman. "Little cabbage? Is that how you think of me?"

"It is a term of endearment." Fannie smiled. "A nickname of sorts."

"I'd rather be a brussels sprout," Hannah teased.

Fannie laughed and Lucas was relieved that both women were allowing a bit of levity to lighten their spirits.

"Ladies, your escort is ready when you are."

"Give me one more minute, Lucas. I want to ask one of the girls to take a sandwich to Samuel. I know he wouldn't feel like eating a large meal after all the excitement, but he needs something before bed."

She soon returned and Lucas helped both women with their capes.

Opening the kitchen door, he surveyed the landscape, searching for any sign of danger. Once satisfied, he motioned Hannah and Fannie forward. "Let's hurry. We'll take the rear path. Stay close, and alert me if you see anything that doesn't look right."

Overhead the moon peered between the clouds. The night air was cool and Hannah shivered. Lucas wanted to put his arm around her shoulders and draw her close, but he didn't want to embarrass her in front of Fannie. Hannah was a private woman. Plus, he needed to keep his attention on the surroundings instead of her pretty face.

Lucas had to admit that he was acting like a cop again, an undercover cop who dressed Amish. Was this why he had come to Willkommen? To protect a woman with expressive blue eyes and a sweet mouth that turned into an enticing smile?

He had to keep her safe, whether he embraced the Amish faith or not. Her life was more important than his future. Although if things worked out, his future might have bearing on her life. At least, that was his hope.

The next morning Hannah hurried down the stairs of Fannie's home and entered the kitchen just as a *rap-tap-tap* sounded at the door.

"Would you see who that is?" Fannie asked as she leaned over the stove and pulled a tray of golden muffins from the oven.

Hannah peered out the window and saw the young teen who worked at the Amish Store. His black waistcoat hung open and his felt hat sat low on his head. Shaggy blond hair curled around his neck and stuck out around his ears.

She opened the door. The cold morning air swept into the kitchen. "Come in before you let out all the heat."

The teen stepped inside, dutifully removed his hat and nodded to Fannie. "Belinda Lapp's mother said to tell you that Belinda is gone. Something happened in the night."

With a heavy sigh Fannie placed the filled muffin tin on the top of the stove. Wiping her hands on a towel, she turned to Joseph. "Do they know where she could have gone?"

The lad shrugged. "Mrs. Lapp did not tell me and I did not ask."

Yet it seemed to Hannah that the teen was holding something back. "Does Belinda have a boyfriend? Perhaps an *Englisch* boyfriend?"

The boy's shoulders slumped. "Belinda does not talk to me about boyfriends."

"Perhaps not," Hannah said. "Yet often we know more than what we've been told. Is that not right?"

Fannie nodded her agreement. "You must tell us what you know, Joseph. Belinda's well-being depends on finding her. She could be in danger."

"Danger?" The teen took a step back. "I do not think that could be."

"If this boyfriend is not a *gut* man—" Fannie stepped closer. "You remember Rosie Glick?"

He nodded. "She was my sister's age. Someone said they saw her riding in a truck last summer a few weeks after she went missing."

"A truck?" Hannah looked at Fannie. "What kind of truck?"

"The kind that makes deliveries."

"Who told you they had seen Rosie?" Fannie asked.

The teen shrugged.

Fannie leaned closer. "You are not to hold

back information when asked, Joseph. This you know to be true."

He fingered his hat and glanced over his shoulder at the door as if ready to bolt. "I need to go back to the store. Mrs. Lapp tried to work, but she was worried about her daughter. Her hands could not move as fast as her mind, so she went home."

"I'll send someone to help you," Fannie assured him. "But first, tell me the name of the person who saw Rosie."

"His name is Levi Raber."

"I do not know the family. They have a home nearby?"

"On the other side of the mountain, but I do not know where. I met him at the lake last summer. He is a good fisherman. I asked him to show me the bait he used."

"And your discussion turned to Rosie Glick?"

"He asked me if I knew an Amish girl named Rosie who had left the area."

"Levi knew Rosie?" Hannah asked, trying to put the pieces together.

"He had heard about her when she first went missing. He was in town, selling his fish at the market. People were talking. He could not help but overhear."

"If he did not know Rosie, then how did he

recognize her when he saw her?" Fannie asked what Hannah had been thinking.

"He had seen an Amish girl with an *Englisch* man at the lake. They were arguing. The man called her Rosie."

Fannie's brow furrowed. "What were they arguing about?"

"Levi did not tell me."

"The sheriff or one of his deputies needs to talk to Levi," Hannah said. "Does he still go to the lake?"

"I have not seen him during the winter. Perhaps he will return in summer."

"You said he saw Rosie in a truck?" Hannah prompted.

"*Yah*, but another man was with Rosie that time. He had a skinny face and pale skin and red hair."

Hannah's heart lurched. "You're sure that's what he said?"

The boy nodded. "I would not tell a lie."

"I didn't think you would." Hannah needed to find Lucas. "Did Levi say where the truck was headed?"

"It was going up the mountain toward the lodge."

"You're sure?" Hannah asked.

"That is what he said."

Hannah needed to go to the lodge. If Rosie had been seen there, Sarah might be there, as well.

Once the boy left, she turned to Fannie. "Tell me about the lodge."

"It is a resort for the wealthy. Our kitchen supplies them with fresh produce and baked goods. They often bring in guests from Atlanta and the Carolinas. Florida, too. There is hunting. They fish on the lake. There is much to interest *Englisch* men in the area."

"Meaning what, Fannie?"

"Meaning I think there may be more than hunting and fishing that attracts them now, from what Joseph has said. We must tell the sheriff."

"Lucas also needs to know."

Both women grabbed their bonnets and capes and hurried out the door, heading to the inn.

Hannah wanted to visit the lodge. Would Lucas go with her? Or would she have to go alone?

Her first priority was her sister. Hannah had to find Sarah. She had to find her now.

THIRTEEN

"Lucas!"

He turned. Hannah was running toward him, waving her arm to get his attention. She was breathless, her cheeks flushed. She grabbed his hand and could hardly get her words out when they met.

"Joseph knows someone who saw Rosie."

"When?"

"Last summer. On the mountain road that leads to the lodge. She was in a delivery truck." Hannah explained what the boy had shared. "The driver of the delivery van had a slender face, but here's the thing, Lucas…"

She paused, catching her breath. "The driver had red hair."

Hannah gripped his hand even more tightly. "Don't you understand? The man who took Sarah was red-haired and slender. It's the same man. The girls might be at the lodge. I'll get my car. Go there with me."

"I need to talk to Joseph before we do anything."

Together they hurried to the store. Joseph looked worried when he saw them.

"You need to tell me everything you said at Fannie's house," Lucas told the teen.

"I spoke the truth."

"I believe you, but I need more information."

Lucas took the boy into the rear of the store. Hannah joined them there. "Tell me what you learned and who told you," Lucas insisted.

The boy recounted what he had told Hannah.

"How can I find Levi?" Lucas asked when Joseph had shared everything he could remember.

"I do not know."

Frustrated by another dead end, Lucas and Hannah left the store and hurried along the path that led to the inn. When the main walkway split in a number of different directions, she stopped and pointed to the mechanic's shop. "Let's get my keys. We can take my car to the lodge."

Lucas grabbed her hand. "We can't drive there."

"What do you mean?"

"We have to go Amish."

"But—"

"We'll take the buggy, although it won't be an easy ride," he cautioned. "Fannie can get the delivery items ready while I harness Daisy."

"I'll help Fannie."

Lucas made sure both women were safely in the B and B's kitchen before he hurried to the barn. A short time later, he guided the buggy to the inn's side entrance.

Fannie helped load the buggy with the boxes filled with winter vegetables, pies, rolls and loaves of bread. "We will have cakes ready if you wait a bit."

Lucas shook his head. "We need to go now. I want to stop at Belinda's house on the way."

Fannie wrapped a loaf of bread and an apple pie in a plastic bag and handed it to Lucas. "Give this to her mother. Tell Lydia we are praying for her daughter's safety. I understand why she could not stay at work today. Tell her to come back when she can. Until then we will ask *Gott* to keep her daughter safe."

Lucas appreciated Fannie's thoughtfulness. "You have a generous heart, Fannie."

"*Yah*, and you are hoping there will be pie left when you return."

He laughed and hugged her, something he rarely did.

The older woman blushed and patted his arm. "You will have me with tears in my eyes for your thoughtfulness. Now go with *Gott* and be careful."

Fannie held out her arms for Hannah. "Be watchful, my child. And remember Amish women do not talk to strangers. Lower your gaze if you come near someone. The bonnet will protect you from being identified. Lucas will keep you safe."

The two women embraced. "Now go," Fannie said, motioning them toward the buggy.

Taking her into his arms, Lucas lifted Hannah into the seat. He couldn't help but note how light she was and how pleasing she smelled. She may be wearing Amish clothing, but she was anything but plain.

Climbing in beside her, he flipped the reins. "Let's go, Daisy."

The mare trotted along the drive and headed for the entrance. Turning onto the main road, Daisy picked up speed. Lucas's heart grew heavy as he thought of what was before them. Hopefully having Hannah accompany him to the lodge wouldn't be a mistake. She might see things he could overlook. Two sets of eyes were always better than one.

His thoughts turned to Olivia. They had been a good team and worked well together, but in the weeks before her death their relationship had changed. Another mistake he had made. He had started to see Olivia as more than a cop. He'd seen her as a woman who had woven her way into his heart.

The ride to the Lapp farm didn't take long. Turning into the drive, Lucas was overcome with a sense of sorrow. Something had happened to Belinda Lapp, he felt sure. The forlorn look on Lydia's face when she stepped onto the porch only confirmed what he was feeling. Her eyes were red. No doubt, she'd been crying.

"Fannie wanted you to have this," he said, handing her the baked goods and wishing he could do something to ease her pain.

"I could not work today because—" The woman's mouth twisted with emotion.

"Stay home as long as you need to," Lucas assured her. "Fannie understands. She sends her love and her prayers."

"She is a good woman, *yah*?"

Lydia was a good woman, too, but her daughter could have been lured into something that might prove deadly.

Lucas's gut tightened as he turned Daisy back to the main road.

Hannah's silence told him that she, too, had been touched deeply by the fear written so plainly on Lydia Lapp's tearstained face. Neither of them spoke for some time and the significance of another young woman gone missing hung heavy between them. Perhaps, Lucas silently mused, it was better if they didn't give voice—at least for a while—to the reality of what had been happening in this once peaceful mountain paradise.

The falling temperature brought both of them back to the present. Hannah wrapped a lap blanket around their legs, then tugged the bonnet down around her forehead and clutched the black cape tightly across her shoulders.

The day was cold and the sky overhead looked ominous.

"It might rain," he warned, grateful for something to talk about that didn't have anything to do with missing women.

"We will not melt if we get wet," she said with an encouraging smile.

He appreciated her straightforwardness. There was nothing weak about Hannah. She could handle any problem, seemingly. Independent maybe to a fault, but he liked women who were assertive and could take care of themselves. Not that he wanted Hannah to take care of herself. He wanted to be there with her, helping her and protecting her.

He jostled the reins and the horse took off along the road.

If only he could keep Hannah safe.

* * *

Riding along the mountain road with Lucas would have been perfect except for the reason they were traveling. Another young woman had gone missing. Hannah needed to find Sarah, but she also worried about Belinda.

As much as she wanted to believe the young Amish girl could be found, Hannah wasn't sure of anything, except Lydia Lapp's sorrow that had tugged at her heart. Some pain was almost too hard to bear. Didn't scripture say that the Lord gave only as much as someone could carry? Surely scripture was mistaken when it came to parents and their children.

She glanced at the rugged mountain terrain and the steep slope of the road ahead. The mare was strong but would she be agile enough on the back path Lucas said they would travel? Hannah wrapped the cape more tightly around her chest.

"You're cold." His glance was laced with concern. "If we were riding in your Nissan, I could turn up the heater. Scoot closer to me, Hannah. Body heat is the only solution."

"I'm fine." But she wasn't. She was worried and frightened about what they might find in spite of her attempt to be strong. Plus, although she didn't want to admit it to Lucas, she *was* cold.

Being Amish in Fannie's warm home with the

rich smells of fresh-baked biscuits and a wood fire to make piping-hot coffee was one thing. Being out in the elements made her have second thoughts about the *plain* life and what she would have to give up if she joined the faith.

The thought took her by surprise. Consciously she hadn't considered embracing the bonnet. She touched the ties under her chin as if to adjust the covering, but her thoughts took in the simplicity of the Amish way, of not having to worry about what she would wear or the need to be in style or to apply makeup or to go to a salon for her hair. All of that seemed so frivolous and such a waste of time when two young women were in danger.

Lucas placed the reins in his left hand and stretched his right hand into the seat behind them. He pulled a thick lap quilt out of a heavy burlap tote and draped it over Hannah's lap.

"The quilt will add more warmth than the blanket alone," he told her. "If you're going to live like the Amish, you need to learn from them. They have warm woolen stockings and undergarments to ward off the cold. They also have outerwear and thick quilts and woolen blankets that insulate them from the frigid temperatures."

"How did you learn so much about their way of life in such a short few months?"

"It was Fannie. She made sure that I was fully immersed in Amish life. Some days I longed to catch up on the local news or find out what was going on in the world at large. She told me I had to decide whether to be of the world or not."

"And you ended up embracing the Amish way?"

"I was hurt when I came here and quite literally stumbled onto the inn. My car had a flat tire half a mile from the entrance. I had seen a small sign at the last intersection I had passed, so I hoofed it there as best I could with an injured leg."

He reached down and touched his old wound, grateful it had healed. "The first week I rented a room in the inn, but I soon got tired of having nothing to do. Calvin fixed my tire. I was ready to drive away, but I didn't know where I'd go. My life had been a jumble of confusion at that point. Fannie had a knack for seeing beneath the surface. She needed help maintaining the property and offered me a job."

"And you moved into the *grossdaadi* house."

Lucas nodded. "That's right. I sold my car to one of the kitchen staff who was going to college in the fall and needed transportation."

"Fannie had convinced you to accept the Amish way?" Hannah asked.

"To at least give it a try."

Hannah smiled. "She said you're like a son to her."

Lucas's gaze softened. "Hearing that makes me happy. She can be tough when she needs to be, but she forced me to work through some of my struggle. I said it was her chicken soup that healed me, but it was her big heart that made the difference. My extended family was scattered. My parents passed when I was young. Having a home had meant a one-bedroom rental."

Hannah nodded. "I can relate."

"She enjoys having you around," he added.

"How can you tell?"

"After eleven months, I can read her almost as well as she can read me. She's been cooking and humming and smiling more recently. I know you're the reason."

He put his arm around her shoulders and pulled her closer. "Feeling warmer?"

"Much. Thank you."

Hannah appreciated Lucas's concern for her comfort. He seemed to be adept with the horse and buggy and with the various ways the Amish would attack any problem.

"You're planning to become Amish?" she asked.

"It's been my hope."

"Do I hear a reservation?"

"Not from me, but the bishop is a different story. He doesn't think I'm ready."

"There's a stumbling block?"

Lucas nodded. "You could say that. Probably has to do with my pride. At least, that's what he led me to believe."

"Pride can be a stumbling block to a lot of things." Hannah thought of her pain when she'd learned about her father. The shock had taken her aback. Her mother's delivery had made the information even more hurtful and her pride had been wounded when she'd found out the truth.

"You don't seem like you have a problem with pride." Lucas jostled the reins and nudged the mare forward.

"Rejection, abandonment—both of those can be overscored with pride when you think you don't deserve to be treated in a certain way."

"You're talking about a guy who didn't appreciate you for who you are," he said as if reading her thoughts.

"That's not too far from the truth." Her mother hadn't made good decisions when it came to men. Hannah's father was proof of that, but she wouldn't go that far back with Lucas. "A seemingly nice guy kept showing up at the store where I worked. He invited me out for coffee. We got to know each other and hit it off, or so I thought."

She glanced at the hillside, trying to find her words. She hadn't talked about Brian to anyone. Maybe sharing some of what had happened would help her heal. "I enjoyed his attention and the nice things he did for me. Brian seemed concerned and attentive. Turns out it was a game for him. He…he lied to me about a number of things. He said a bill from his credit-card company had gotten lost in the mail. His late payment hurt his credit. He asked to use one of my credit cards to buy supplies for the law office where he worked. He assured me he'd be able to pay me back."

A muscle in Lucas's neck tensed. He kept his eyes on the road. Perhaps he thought her gullible and naive. Seemed she was both.

"Of course, he didn't plan to pay me back," she admitted. "He charged a number of big-ticket items to my card that didn't pertain to his job and seemed hurt when I questioned him. He made up another excuse and then another. Finally, I did some investigating and found an address that he hadn't told me about."

Lucas squeezed her hand, offering support.

"I went there when I thought he was home from work. We had always met in town. I thought he shared a house with two other guys, but the guy who came to the door was five years old. The child's mother appeared and then the child's father did, as well."

Lucas wrapped his arm around her shoulders. "It was Brian?"

She nodded. "I never suspected that he was married. He was using me the entire time. Here's the funny thing. He told me he worked for a well-established law firm in Atlanta. Turns out he's an ambulance chaser and not a good one. But he said if I made a fuss, he'd make certain that people would think I stole money from him." Which was a repeat of what had happened in her own home.

Hannah hung her head in shame. His hateful words echoed through her mind. *I know who your father is. Once the information is made public, your reputation will be ruined. No one will believe anything you say.*

"I'm sorry, Hannah. You were too good for him."

"Too stupid is what I was, but I learned my lesson, that's for sure."

"Did you go to the police?"

Inwardly she flinched. How could she explain her reason for not notifying the authorities? "I... I worried that he would discredit my reputation and my credit."

"So you did nothing?"

"I moved to Macon. I turned off my cell

phone and got a prepaid cell to use instead. I changed email addresses in case he tried to contact me over the internet. I didn't want him to find me."

"You weren't the one at fault."

"I wasn't sure how he would spin the story, and I couldn't risk what he might do."

"You need to let law enforcement know."

She shook her head. "It's all right, Lucas. That part of my life has ended."

"That's why you don't want to go back to Macon," he said, which wasn't far from the truth.

"Do you think I'm foolish?" she asked.

"Not at all. I think he bullied you and badgered you and told you untruths. I can help you."

"It's okay, really."

"But you have property there, your household furnishings, clothing."

"Nothing of value."

He stared at her, probably wondering why she had accumulated so little in her life.

"When you grow up with a mother who never stayed long in any one place, you learn to travel light. Anything we acquired that brought joy or comfort to our lives had to be left behind when she awakened us, often in the middle of the night, to climb into the car and leave for someplace new."

"What about your education? A kid would have to be smart to get by in that type of situation."

"Maybe, or maybe it worked because we were young. We didn't know any other way to live. We never established strong friendships because we always had to say goodbye."

"I'm sorry, Hannah. You and your sisters should have been close."

"You would have thought we would be, but Mother manipulated us with her love and played us one against the other. Especially Miriam and me. Miriam was the dutiful daughter. I dreamed of making my own way." She laughed ruefully. "And look what happened to me. You might say that I've become my mother."

"You can't believe that."

"I've been wandering through life, which is what my mother always did. She was searching for something, although I never knew what it was."

"Maybe love and acceptance," Lucas suggested.

"That was something her daughters couldn't give her."

"Of course not. You needed her to mother you and provide the love and acceptance you needed. Don't confuse the roles here, Hannah.

The child is never the one who needs to take care of the mother."

"But Miriam did."

"Later in life, but not when you were growing up."

Hannah picked at the cape and lowered her head. She didn't want to talk about her childhood or her mother or her dysfunctional life. Nor did she want to consider what her life could have been like if she hadn't been so gullible when it came to Brian. She had been such a fool.

She scooted away from Lucas, needing to distance herself from his warmth and acceptance. She had made a mistake in Atlanta when she had given her heart to the wrong man. She wouldn't, she couldn't, make that same mistake again.

FOURTEEN

Lucas turned the buggy onto the narrow mountain path that led to the lodge. Hannah had been silent and lost in her own memories ever since she'd mentioned the man in Atlanta. From what she'd said, it sounded as if she still cared for Brian.

So many thoughts swirled through Lucas's mind that centered on pride and betrayal and abandonment. His world had ended in Savannah when Olivia died, but he'd gone after the shipping magnate and his company. The guy was well connected and his goons and minions had soon come after Lucas. He never would have backed off except for the suitcase uncovered in Olivia's personal effects and the immediate supposition that she was involved in something criminal. Olivia had never been dirty, but money didn't lie. At least, that was what his supervisor warned. The stash of marked bills had made her a suspect in a Savannah murder-for-hire case.

Lucas was thought to have been dirty by association, and he'd been encouraged, rather forcefully, to resign from the force before he was incriminated, as well.

Turning in his badge had been a necessity, but he hadn't given up. He'd followed one last lead to Willkommen, where Vipera was said to have had holdings in the Pine Lodge Mountain Resort. An allegation Lucas could never prove.

Thankfully his search had led to the Amish Inn. God had wanted him to accept healing instead of vengeance. Although now Lucas wasn't sure he had read God correctly.

The back road around the mountain was bumpy and rough. Hannah bounced from side to side.

"Hold on," he warned. His hands held tightly to the reins when he wanted to wrap his arm protectively around Hannah. She was in another world, a world of memories, probably about the man who had stolen her heart. Lucas wouldn't interfere. She needed time to work out her past just as he had.

"We're almost to the lodge," he finally said. "We'll be watchful but appear to be minding our own business."

The buggy crested a small rise and the lodge

was visible in the distance. Pretentiously grand, the stone structure rose like a sturdy fortress, and its windows gleamed golden from the reflection of the sun that broke momentarily through the clouds.

The three-story resort had a circular drive that passed under an A-frame portico at the entrance. From what Lucas had heard, many a person of prominence, whether in the sports world, business or entertainment, had visited the resort for a relaxing respite. Their privacy was protected above all else. Security guards wearing gray, down-filled jackets bearing the name of the resort patrolled the grounds to keep unwanted visitors from encroaching on the premises.

"We might be stopped as we near the lodge," he warned. "Let me do the talking."

A small security guardhouse stood to the left of the entrance road. A man wearing a gray jacket and metallic, wraparound sunglasses stepped from the protective structure. He raised his hand to stop the buggy.

Lucas pulled back on the reins and nodded to the bulky guy packing heat. "We are making a delivery from the Amish Inn," he informed the man.

"What's in your buggy?"

"Produce and baked goods."

The guard peered at the stack of boxes in the rear of the buggy and then pointed to the narrow road that curved around the side of the large stone structure. "Take that path to the right. It leads to the kitchen entrance. Someone will help you unload."

"Danke."

With a flip of the reins, Lucas guided Daisy onto the narrow side road. He glanced at the front entrance where another muscle-bound guy stood guard and wondered whether Hannah realized that both men in the security detail were heavily armed.

They rounded the side of the lodge and stopped at the entrance to the kitchen. In the distance, Lucas spotted a row of cottages nestled in a wooded area beyond the well-landscaped lawn. Although rustic in appearance, each seemed artistically decorated in accord with the resort's five-star rating. Perhaps guests who wanted a special getaway could rent the cottages to be one with nature, as the brochures for the resort probably stated.

Secluded luxury. But something else was underfoot. Lucas could sense the tension in the air. What was really happening at the lodge?

"¡Hola!"

A woman opened the door to the kitchen and

hurried outside to greet them. "You are bringing us baked goods, yes?" She was short and plump, with a strong Hispanic accent.

"Pies and bread and root vegetables that just came from some of our local farms," he said with enthusiasm.

"This is good. We are opening soon after our renovation."

Hannah nodded in greeting and then followed Lucas's lead and climbed from the buggy.

"My name is Isabella," the woman said as she quickly reached for one of the boxes. "I will help you unload."

Lucas handed Hannah a smaller box containing pies and cookies, and hefted the heavier produce box into his own arms.

The inviting smell of a hearty soup, simmering on the stove, greeted them when they entered the state-of-the-art kitchen. Hannah glanced at the pair of stainless-steel refrigerators, the granite countertops and copper pots. If the kitchen was this grand, she could only imagine the ambience in the areas of the lodge open to the guests.

Another Hispanic woman, shorter than Isabella, unpacked the pies and nodded her approval as she placed them on one of the far counters.

"Hurry, Maria," Isabella encouraged. "There are more boxes to unload."

The smaller woman had no problem lifting the heavier cartons and the buggy was soon empty.

"I'll need a signature," Lucas said, holding out an invoice form.

"Yes." Isabella nodded. "You have not been here before?"

Lucas shook his head. "You'll have to direct me."

"I will take you to the food and beverage director's office. It is just down the hall."

She hurried Lucas out of the kitchen, leaving Hannah to enjoy the succulent aromas.

Maria appeared younger and more timid than Isabella, but she smiled sweetly to Hannah and pointed to the coffeepot. "You would like coffee? Maybe tea?"

As much as Hannah appreciated the offer, she declined and stared through the window at the cottages. "It's beautiful here. So many wealthy people must visit."

"*Sí*, is beautiful." The woman picked up a long-handled spoon and stirred the soup.

Hannah stepped closer. "Maria, I need information. Have you by any chance seen an Amish girl? She's sixteen and dressed like I am."

The woman's neck tensed.

"She's from the local area but has gone missing."

The woman dropped the spoon. The utensil clattered on the granite.

"She's a nice girl," Hannah continued, "but she got involved with an older man."

The woman flicked a sideways glance at Hannah and then turned to pull a gallon of milk from the refrigerator.

"Do you understand me?" Hannah asked. "The girl's name is Belinda?"

"No hablo inglés," the woman insisted as she poured milk into a large measuring cup.

Hannah doubted the woman's inability to speak English since she had offered coffee and had readily followed her supervisor's instructions to unload the buggy.

"My sister is missing, as well," Hannah continued, unwilling to be deterred. "Sarah is twenty-one and blonde. She disappeared six weeks ago. She might be with a tall, slender, red-haired man who is thought to be holding her captive. Plus, a girl disappeared eight months ago. Her name is Rosie."

The woman turned worried eyes to Hannah. Then, glancing down, she opened her mouth as if to speak.

At that moment Isabella stepped back into the kitchen.

"Your friend will be here soon," she assured Hannah. "He is waiting for the director to return to his office."

Isabella glared at the younger woman. "Maria, you are making pudding?"

"*Sí.*" She returned the milk to the refrigerator.

Isabella smiled at Hannah. "Perhaps you would like coffee?"

"No, thank you. Maria already asked me." Hannah touched the younger woman's shoulder. "Was there something else you wanted to tell me?"

Once again Maria lowered her gaze. "No, senorita."

Realizing Maria wouldn't divulge anything within earshot of her boss, Hannah pointed to the door. "I'll wait outside near the buggy."

She shivered when she left the kitchen. Not from the cold mountain air but from the sense of foreboding that permeated the setting. Maria had something to say. If only Isabella hadn't returned so soon.

Rounding the buggy, Hannah gazed at a cluster of cottages sitting on the opposite side of the landscaped lawn. On the far right, a cobblestone path led past a wooded area and then on to one cottage secluded from the rest. Hannah glanced back at the kitchen, seeing both women huddled over the central work island with their backs to the windows.

She peered at the sun peeking through the

clouds and decided a stroll to stretch her legs would be good before the ride home.

A breeze picked at her skirt and made her grab her black bonnet before it flew off her head. She again glanced back, relieved that no one seemed to notice her ambling along the path. The stone pavement led through an area shaded by tall pines. A chill settled over her and she pulled the cape tighter, knowing she should turn around, yet her gaze was drawn to the cottage that appeared to be constructed from hand-hewed logs.

Lace curtains hung at the windows and rustic rockers and pots of pansies decorated the wraparound porch. All of which looked inviting.

A flicker of movement behind the curtain on the far right window caught Hannah's attention. Someone was looking out. Perhaps one of the guests renting the accommodations or a housekeeper tidying up the room.

Before Hannah could turn and retrace her steps, the curtain pulled back ever so slightly and a face peered from the window. A teenage girl's face.

Even at this distance Hannah could see her wide eyes and sad frown. She could also see the bodice of her blue dress and the ties of a white bonnet that hung around her neck.

Hannah started toward the cabin when a hand grabbed her arm. "What do you think you're doing, lady?"

She turned, seeing the snarling face of one of the guards. His nostrils flared and the anger flashing from his eyes bored into her.

"You're trespassing on private property."

"But—"

Hannah glanced over her shoulder. The curtain had dropped into place. No one remained at the window.

"Are you interfering with our guests?" the man demanded.

Hannah hung her head and pulled in a silent prayer. She needed to appear meek, humble and authentically Amish. "Forgive me, sir. I was waiting outside and the path invited me to walk before my buggy ride home."

He jerked her forward and growled his frustration. "You folks live by your own set of rules, but we've got rules here that need to be obeyed. Now hurry along and get back to your buggy."

Hannah pulled her arm free and ran, wanting to distance herself from the hateful man.

She also needed to tell Lucas about what she had seen at the cabin.

Not what, she corrected herself, but who.

She had seen Belinda, the missing Amish girl.

FIFTEEN

Lucas flipped the reins, encouraging the mare to increase her pace. Hannah peered back at the lodge.

"I don't see anyone following us," she said, breathing a sigh of relief.

"What happened, Hannah? Your face is pale as death and you're still trembling."

She quickly explained about the small cottage and the face at the window.

"It was her, Lucas. It was Belinda. She was peering through a window from the cottage on the right, closest to the wooded area."

"Are you sure about what you saw? I didn't think you had even met Belinda."

She straightened her spine. "I haven't. But the girl was wearing a blue dress. White ribbons hung around her neck."

"That doesn't mean it was Belinda Lapp." As much as he appreciated Hannah's desire to rescue the girl, Lucas wasn't convinced the girl at the window—whoever she was—needed rescuing. "Did the guard realize someone had been at the window?"

"I doubt he noticed the girl. He was probably more concerned about the Amish woman—namely me—trespassing on private property."

She grabbed Lucas's arm. "We have to go back and try to save Belinda."

Lucas blew out a deep breath. "We're not the ones, Hannah. It needs to be law enforcement."

"Belinda is in the cottage. I'm sure of it."

"That may be, but she could be there of her own volition."

Hannah let out a frustrated breath. "She's sixteen."

"I know, but we need to be prudent."

"Prudent I agree with, but I think we're being foolish to leave her behind. Besides, Sarah could be there, as well."

"If we go back, the guard will stop us. I know he frightened you, Hannah. He would be even more antagonistic if he realized you had returned."

"Then what can we do?"

"First things first. You'll stay with Fannie while I talk to the sheriff."

"We'll both talk to the sheriff." She steeled her jaw and released hold of his arm, then turned to stare at the road ahead.

As much as Lucas wanted Belinda and Sarah and Rosie to be found and brought to safety, he knew going back without law enforcement would be a risky mistake. Plus, the girl at the window could be the teenage daughter of one of the guests or even a worker at the lodge.

Seth and Simon Keim had considered applying for a job at the resort. Perhaps housekeeping used Amish girls, as well. Racing headlong into a cottage because of a nebulous figure at the window, who had made no attempt to signal for help, seemed brash. Although he wouldn't use that term with Hannah. Her heart was in the right place for sure.

"When I was in the food director's office, I saw a memo on his desk," Lucas shared. "Seems a number of important people are arriving late tonight in anticipation of the big opening. Someone from the sheriff's office needs to pull surveillance and find out who those important folks are and whether they have ties to any illegal operations in other areas of the state."

"And what about the girl I saw at the window?"

"Surveillance will watch for anyone going or coming, Hannah, including young women in blue dresses."

Hannah seemed satisfied with his response, for which Lucas was grateful. Feeling a swell of relief when they arrived back at the inn, he stopped the buggy at the kitchen entrance and hurriedly unloaded the boxes.

Fannie met them there. "Did you find anything of interest?"

Lucas looked at Hannah. "Maybe. We're going to talk to the sheriff and let him decide how to proceed."

He handed Fannie the signed invoice. "Any news on Belinda?"

"Nothing new. Joseph's brother is helping at the store but both boys need to go home soon."

"Lucas?" Hannah rushed toward him and held out a scrap of paper. "I found this stuck in the corner of one of the empty produce boxes."

His gut tightened when he read the note. *I see Amish girl last night.*

"Maria wrote the note," Hannah insisted. "She started to tell me something before Isabella came back into the kitchen."

"I'll talk to the sheriff."

Hannah hurried after him. "Not without me."

"And me," Fannie said, following behind them.

Sheriff Kurtz had been reading the newspaper in the easy chair. At least, that was what he told them when he opened the door and invited them into his room, although his eyes were puffy and he appeared to have been napping.

"I'm sorry we had to disturb you," Lucas said. "But there's information you need to know."

Hannah quickly explained what she had seen and about the guard who had stopped her on the path, as well as the note she'd found.

"There are a number of security guards on-site and they're armed," Lucas said.

The sheriff rubbed his chin. "Seems strange to have all that protection unless some well-known guest is staying there."

Lucas nodded. "A few VIPs are arriving late tonight, according to the memo I saw. If we can identify them, we might learn what's really going on at the lodge."

"It's been closed for renovation and opens this weekend," Fannie shared.

"Security is tight because of the women they're holding captive in the cottage," Hannah insisted.

"One woman," Lucas corrected.

"One that we know about," she admitted. "Although there could be more."

"If a couple of your deputies pull surveillance," Lucas told the sheriff, "we might be able to identify who those people of prominence are and whether they have ties to illegal activity. Tell your guys to watch for any young women escorted by older men who don't appear to be related."

"Sounds like a good plan." The sheriff reached for his cell. "I'll call Deputy Gainz and pass the information on to him. He'll check it out."

Which didn't seem to appease Hannah, from the way she sighed with frustration. "He'd better hurry before they transport Belinda to some other hideout."

The sheriff tried to place the call then shook his head. "I can't get service."

"You can use the phone in my office," Fannie suggested.

Even if the sheriff could reach Gainz, the deputy wasn't the most aggressive officer of the law. Could he amass enough manpower to thoroughly search the resort? Lucas couldn't stand idly by after reading the note that mentioned an Amish girl, who could be in danger.

"Sir, I'll go back to the lodge," Lucas said.

The sheriff nodded. "Make sure you don't go empty-handed. Take that Glock I gave you yesterday. You know what to do. I could swear you in as a deputy."

Lucas held up his hand. "That won't be necessary."

"I'll call Gainz and let him know you'll need backup. I'll also tell him to have at least one of our guys keeping track of arrivals and departures. Maybe we'll be able to hook some big fish." The sheriff put his hand on Fannie's shoulder and leaned on her as they left the room.

Hannah stared at him. "What's going on, Lucas?"

"You wanted me to go back for Belinda."

"But not as a deputy," she insisted. "You're not law enforcement."

"I was in Savannah."

She took a step back. "What are you saying?"

"It's the reason I came here. My partner, Olivia Parker, was killed. She was working on a trafficking investigation that could have incriminated a local shipping tycoon. His name's Vipera and he's supposed to be connected to the lodge, at least financially. Only nothing materialized until today. If women are being trafficked as that note could indicate, he might be involved."

"Then this is more about you getting even rather than trying to save Belinda."

"What?" He didn't understand her logic.

For all Hannah's earlier insistence that he needed to rescue the Amish girl, she now seemed totally against him doing just that.

"You're Amish, Lucas."

He shook his head. "I'm not."

"Isn't it what you want for your life?"

"I was wrong."

"No, you weren't, but now you think the person who killed your partner is suddenly involved and that gives you a reason to throw away your future. Is it that pride we talked about? Or is it the desire to avenge her death that you've grappled with all this time?"

He felt betrayed. "Evildoers need to be stopped."

"Stopped and brought to justice, but not stopped dead in their tracks."

"What are you insinuating, Hannah?"

"You're going back in hopes of finding the man who killed your partner or was in some way responsible for your partner's death. Her name was Olivia, right? When she died, did your dreams of a life together die, as well?"

"You don't know what you're talking about."

"Don't I? I can see it in your eyes, Lucas. It's why you were a broken man when you came here."

"I was broken because of taking a bullet to my leg," he insisted. " I told you Fannie nursed me back to health."

"And Fannie told you to forget the past and live a new life, to let go of the world and embrace the Amish way."

"That's what I've tried to do."

"But you failed, Lucas, because of the need for revenge that's hardened your heart."

"It's called justice, Hannah."

The sheriff's laptop was open on the desk.

She tapped Lucas's name into the search-engine bar and quickly read the headers that appeared on the screen. "The Savannah paper seems to have a number of articles with you in the title. Let's look at this one." She clicked on the link.

"Hannah, you're being irrational."

"Am I?" The news article appeared on the screen.

"'Sergeant Lucas Grant is thought to be involved…his partner was implicated…marked bills were found in Officer Olivia Parker's apartment,'" Hannah read aloud, catching the high points of the piece. "'An unnamed source claims Parker may have been involved in a criminal activity, involving bribery and money laundering. Her partner, Sergeant Lucas Grant, denies the allegations.'"

Hannah glanced at Lucas and then back at the monitor as she continued to read. "'Another source stated that Sergeant Lucas Grant might be involved in the corruption, as well. He turned in his badge and is on medical leave. The spokesperson claims there is speculation that his career in law enforcement is over and that he, too, will be indicted if their investigation goes to court.'"

She looked up and glared at him. "I keep making the same mistake."

"What do you mean?" He stepped closer.

"I keep getting involved with the wrong type of men."

Calvin rapped on the open door. "Sorry to interrupt you, folks, but Joseph needs help at the store. Is anyone available?"

"I'll go," Hannah volunteered.

"No, wait." Lucas grabbed her arm. "We need to talk this out."

"You've already made up your mind, Lucas." She hurried from the room.

Lucas started to follow but Fannie stopped him in the hallway. "Calvin will protect her. She'll be safe, but I don't think you will be. I know what you're planning. It's not wise. As much as I want to see Belinda saved, this is a line you should not cross."

"I can't sit by when someone is in danger. These men need to be apprehended."

"You're one person, Lucas. You cannot take them all down. I know you, and I can read your heart. You have not changed since Savannah. You're still intent on stopping the people who killed your partner."

"I'm intent on saving a young woman held captive."

Lucas left the inn and ran toward the mechanic's shed, where he grabbed the keys to Hannah's car. He climbed behind the wheel, started the engine and pulled onto the roadway. As he neared the Amish Store, Joseph came running out. His cheek was bruised and his lip bloodied. Calvin stumbled to the doorway, holding his head.

Lucas sprang from the car. "What happened?"

"A man. He knocked Calvin out and grabbed Hannah. He said he recognized her even in her Amish clothing. He said if Miriam could not be found, he would have to make do with her."

"Where did he take her?"

"I do not know," the boy said. "But he drove away in a delivery truck."

"Get medical help for Calvin and tell the sheriff that I'm going to the lodge."

Lucas accelerated out of the yard and turned right. He'd take the narrow back road. If Daisy could pull the buggy around the mountain, Hannah's car could handle the rough terrain, as well.

He thought of Olivia dead on the pavement because he had arrived too late. He had to find Hannah. He had to find her in time.

SIXTEEN

Lucas drove like a madman up the hill and turned onto the shortcut that rounded the mountain and led to the lodge.

"Lord, help me," he prayed aloud. "I need to find Hannah."

His heart beat against his chest and sent a ripple of fear to weave along his spine.

He couldn't live if something happened to Hannah. "Please, Lord."

As he neared the spot where the path intersected with the main road, Lucas flipped off the headlights. He turned right onto a narrow trail that wove through a wooded area. After backing into a small clearing surrounded by trees, he cut the engine and stepped from the car.

Pausing for a moment, he listened for any sound that could alert him to Hannah's whereabouts before making his way, carefully and quietly, through the undergrowth. Drawing close to the resort, he stopped and stared for a long moment to study the stone building, the kitchen doorway and the cottages in the distance.

Hannah had mentioned a more secluded cottage nestled to the right at the edge of the woods. He moved through the underbrush until the small lodging came into view. A light shone in the front bay window as well as a window at the side of the cottage, no doubt where Hannah had seen the girl's face.

The main structure of the lodge sat dark and foreboding with only a few rooms lit on the first floor. In contrast, the landscaped walkways had recessed lighting tucked in the shrubbery and along the paths, painting the grounds in a surreal glow. How could an area so lovely harbor anything as evil as human trafficking?

Though eager to find Hannah, Lucas also knew going in blind would be a mistake.

His gut tightened. What if she wasn't there? Suppose the man in the blue hoodie had taken her someplace else? What if they were on the highway headed for Atlanta or Savannah? Lucas's hand fisted and he touched the weapon strapped to his hip.

Headlights appeared on the main mountain road. He moved closer to the edge of the tree line to get a better view of the road and felt a sense of relief when a beige delivery truck pulled into sight. The guy in flannel had taken the longer route through Willkommen, which allowed Lucas to arrive first.

The truck pulled into the drive. A guard waved the vehicle on. The truck skirted the kitchen and turned onto the side road that led to the small cottage.

The front door of the cottage opened. A man, dressed in the black slacks and gray jacket uniform of the security team, stepped onto the porch. He waited until the truck braked to a stop before he hurried to the driver's side of the vehicle.

The guy in flannel climbed from the truck, rounded to the rear and opened the door. He and the other man peered into the darkened interior.

Lucas stepped closer. A twig snapped underfoot. Both men turned to stare in his direction. Lucas held his breath and chastised himself for his stupidity. In his haste, he had made a mistake that could prove deadly.

As the men watched, an armadillo scurried out of the wooded area and raced across the path. The guy in flannel laughed before they both turned back to the van.

Lucas's heart pounded when he saw what they pulled from the rear. Hannah bound and gagged. She struggled against their hold. Her bonnet was gone and her hair had pulled free from her bun.

His pulse raced and he wanted to rush forward to save her. Before he stepped from the shadows, something caught his eye on the distant path. Two security agents walked toward the lodge, oblivious to what was happening at the cottage.

The guy in flannel untied the rope binding her legs and then shoved Hannah up the stairs of the porch. She tripped and fell. The sound of her knees hitting the steps ripped through Lucas's heart.

Her kidnapper jerked her upright and pushed her toward the door. She stumbled inside. The guard, who had been inside earlier, followed her into the cottage.

The flannel guy returned to the delivery truck, started the engine and drove around the far side of the lodge. The sound of the engine faded in the distance.

Lucas scanned the property, searching for any sign of security. Seeing no one, he approached the cottage, flattened his back against the wood siding and inched his way toward the window. Curtains covered the panes, but a slit between the panels provided a tiny view into the room.

A voice sounded, moving toward the window.

Lucas ducked just as the curtain was pulled back. Huddled only inches below the window, he held his breath.

The voice became more muffled.

Lucas waited until he heard nothing and then, ever so slightly, raised his head and peered over the edge of the windowsill.

His heart stopped.

He saw Belinda Lapp on a bed. Her hair was disheveled, but from the rise and fall of her shoulders, she appeared to be breathing evenly. Hopefully she was unharmed.

The door to the bedroom opened and Hannah appeared. Her mouth was gagged and her wrists bound.

Her eyes widened ever so slightly. Had she seen him?

She struggled against the guard's hold. He raised his hand and slapped her face.

Lucas felt the blow to his heart as if he had been the one struck. If only it could have been directed at him instead of Hannah.

The guard shoved her onto a straight-back chair and retied the rope around her ankles. He raised his voice. Lucas couldn't make out the words, but from the harsh tone, the guard's displeasure was evident. A door inside the cottage slammed.

Minutes later the front door opened. Lucas peered around the corner and watched the guard jog to the lodge.

Lucas had to move quickly, but before he could move, two more security guys appeared on the path.

Were they heading to the lodge? Or coming for Hannah?

Hannah's heart beat so hard she thought it would surely beat out of her chest. Although terrified by the guards and the man in flannel who had brought her here, she was even more unsettled by the face at the window.

Had it been Lucas or a figment of her imagination?

Tears filled her eyes. She blinked them away. She couldn't cry now. She had to remain focused on what was happening around her.

The Amish girl lay on the bed. Asleep or drugged, Hannah wasn't sure.

Keeping her feet together, she raised her legs and kicked the mattress once and then struck the bed again and again. The exertion made her breathless. She struggled to pull enough air into her lungs. Frustrated, she bit into the gag, wishing she could rip it in two and be rid of the hateful restraint.

The cloth slipped ever so slightly. Using her chin and shoulder, she tugged at the fabric until her lips were free. Opening her mouth, she pulled in a deep breath, filling her lungs with sweet air.

Buoyed by her success, she kicked the bed again and wiggled her hands back and forth in the hope of releasing the rope that bound her wrists. The coarse hemp dug into her flesh, but she ignored the pain.

She scooted to the edge of the chair for better leverage and slowly raised herself to a standing position, then hopped forward and dropped onto the bed.

Using her bound hands, Hannah gripped Belinda's arm and jerked. The girl's eyes blinked open.

Relieved, Hannah leaned closer. "I'm from the inn. You've got to wake up. We have to get away."

The girl moaned.

Not to be daunted, Hannah jostled her again. "Open your eyes, Belinda. We're in danger and have to escape."

The girl blinked, appearing dazed. She stared at Hannah for a long moment then tried to sit up. "Save…save me," she whispered.

"I will, but I need your help." Hannah held out her hands. "Undo the rope."

The girl pulled herself up and grimaced as she fumbled with the restraint. "It is knotted so tightly."

"Maybe there's something in the bathroom." Hannah pointed to the adjoining bath.

Holding on to the bed frame, Belinda struggled to her feet and stumbled forward while Hannah lifted up a silent prayer.

The girl returned to the bed carrying a small plastic case. "I found a nail file and scissors."

Which wouldn't hold up against the thick rope. Hannah's spirits fell, but she held out her hands nonetheless.

Belinda didn't try to cut the sturdy hemp. Instead she snipped at each individual thread. Amazed, Hannah watched as, little by little, the rope frayed. She tugged against the remaining strands that eventually broke free.

Hannah rubbed her wrists and then undid her legs.

"We have to hurry," she told Belinda.

The outside door opened and footsteps sounded in the main room of the cottage.

The girl gripped Hannah's arm. "He's come back."

Before Hannah could respond, the knob turned and the door opened.

* * *

Lucas hadn't expected the look of terror on Hannah's face when he opened the bedroom door.

"Oh, Lucas." She collapsed into his arms. "We thought you were the guard."

"Are you all right?"

She nodded. "Belinda helped me break free of the ropes binding my wrists and legs."

He looked at the girl's dilated pupils. She had been drugged, but the effects appeared to be wearing off.

"We need to leave the cabin now." He squeezed Hannah's hand before he opened the bedroom door. "Follow me."

They hurriedly crossed the living room. Lucas opened the front door ever so slightly and peered outside. Seeing no one, he motioned the women forward.

He kept his eyes on the surrounding area and then followed the women down the porch steps and into the woods.

"The car is parked through there." He pointed to the clearing.

The sound of an engine caused them to turn.

Just as before, a delivery truck braked to a stop in front of the cottage. A man stepped to the pavement. He was dressed in a windbreaker and jeans, and wore a Braves baseball cap over his short-cropped hair. He rounded the truck, opened a side door and jerked a woman onto the pavement. She gasped as he forced her up the steps to the porch. The guy stopped and turned to study the landscape before he shoved her into the cottage.

"The woman—" Hannah grabbed Lucas's arm. "I didn't see her face, but she has blond hair. What if it's Sarah?"

SEVENTEEN

Hannah couldn't take her eyes off the cottage in the hope of catching another glimpse of the blonde woman.

Lucas gently gripped her shoulders and turned her around. "Whether it's Sarah or not, you and Belinda have to get away."

"I can't leave now."

"Think about Belinda's safety. Drive her to the inn and get help. I'll stay here and see what happens."

"What about Deputy Gainz? Wasn't he supposed to be doing surveillance?"

Lucas sighed. "He's probably still in Willkommen."

He pulled the car keys from his pocket and shoved them into her hand. "Go. Now."

She took the keys and then watched as another truck arrived, stopped at the guardhouse and drove to the cottage.

A man climbed from the truck and limped

toward the porch. His phone rang. He stopped to dig it from his pocket and raised it to his ear. "Yeah?"

"It's one of the men from Savannah," Lucas said, his voice low and menacing.

"One of the men who killed your partner?"

He nodded. "I recognize him by the way he walks."

"Are you sure?"

"Of course I'm sure." He motioned Hannah toward the car. "You need to get going before someone sees you."

"What about you?"

"I'm going back, Hannah. He needs to be stopped."

"You can't. There are too many of them and only one of you. Plus, you think vengeance is sweet. You want to kill him for what he did to Olivia. Only that won't get you anywhere. You'll be outnumbered and captured yourself."

She stared at him, trying to read his thoughts. "It won't help Olivia, either."

"But it'll help me, Hannah. It'll help me get over the guilt I've carried for too long and the deep need I have to pay back the injustice done to a woman who didn't deserve to die."

"One injustice doesn't warrant another one. You're hoping to be Amish, but you're not there, and you won't be after this. If you kill that man, you'll be tied up with court hearings. You could end up in jail or, at the very least, you would be pulled back into the world of law enforcement."

"It was the life I knew."

"It tore you apart."

"Then help me heal, Hannah."

She shook her head. "I'm staying at the inn. Fannie can always use an extra pair of hands, and I need a place where I'm accepted for who I am. A place where I don't have to worry about the past or the future. Come with us now, Lucas. We'll send law enforcement to save Sarah or whoever she is."

"I'm not leaving," he insisted.

With a frustrated sigh, Hannah turned and hurried to the car where the girl waited. She had to get help. Lucas was walking into a trap. A trap that would get him killed. As much as she wanted to rescue the blonde woman, Hannah had to help Belinda first.

Sheriff Kurtz would send law enforcement, and not just Deputy Gainz, to free Sarah or whoever the woman might be.

Lord, protect her and protect Lucas.

Hannah had hoped that someday she and Lucas could have a future together and both become Amish and embrace the peace-loving lifestyle that had been healing for both of them, but Lucas was eaten up with vengeance that hardened his heart. He couldn't love her when his thoughts were still on Olivia.

Tears stung Hannah's eyes and her heart nearly broke. She could save Belinda. If only she could save Lucas, as well.

Seeing the man from Savannah brought back the pain Lucas had experienced after Olivia's death. The memories of her body lying on the pavement and her long hair matted with blood caused the anger to return.

His leg ached, reminding him of the gunshot wound and his weeks of recovery. No telling what would have happened to him if it hadn't been for Fannie. She had brought him back to life and to the faith she embraced. Now he was ready to discard everything he had learned about the Amish way and about himself over the past eleven months.

The man still held the cell phone to his ear and talked excitedly to someone on the other end. Lucas turned his head, hoping to catch some snippet of the conversation.

"Vipera." The name of the tycoon from Savannah.

Lucas glanced at the cottage, knowing he was outnumbered and could be easily overpowered by the guards. That wouldn't do the blonde woman any good, nor would it bring Olivia's killers to justice.

Vipera had top-notch lawyers that could adjudicate his release. The tycoon would never stand trial without concrete evidence to substantiate his guilt.

Lucas needed one of his goons to talk.

Slowly and surely, he crept from his hiding spot and crossed the clearing. The guy was still on the phone with his back to the van.

Lucas came up behind him.

Just as he disconnected, Lucas wrapped his arm about the guy's neck and cupped his other hand over his mouth.

"Don't move, and don't make a sound," Lucas whispered.

The guy struggled to break free.

Lucas grabbed the guy's phone and then shoved the Glock into his back. "What don't you understand about not resisting?"

The man stopped moving.

"Remember Olivia Parker, the cop you killed in Savannah?"

The guy shook his head and tried to speak. Lucas's hand pressed even more tightly against his mouth.

"Don't plead innocent," Lucas snarled. "I know you and your buddy killed her. You had orders from Vipera, but you were the one who beat her and then slit her throat."

The guy tried to shake his head. Lucas jammed the gun even deeper into his back until the struggling stopped.

"We're going to take a little walk."

Lucas half dragged, half shoved him around the side of the truck, heading for the underbrush where they'd be hidden from the guards. Before they left the protective cover of the truck, the door to the cottage opened and a guard stepped outside.

Lucas's chest tightened. Where had he come from? There had to be a back door, which made everything much more complicated and dangerous.

"I'll check and see if Xavier took the Amish girls to the lodge," the guard said over his shoulder to someone still inside. His voice traveled in the night. "Call my cell if you learn their whereabouts."

The guard descended the porch steps and hurried along the pavement.

The guy from Savannah jerked. His knee hit the van. The sound broke through the stillness.

Tightening his hold, Lucas pushed him flush against the truck.

The guard turned. He was coming back to the cottage. Lucas had to decide what to do…fast.

EIGHTEEN

Tears stung Hannah's eyes as she drove along the path leading away from the lodge. She didn't turn on the headlights and instead followed the tree line, praying she wouldn't snag the car on a boulder or drop into a rut. Her eyes flicked to the rearview mirror to ensure they weren't being followed.

Thankfully, all she saw was the dark night that swallowed them in its grasp.

"How…how did you find me?" Belinda asked, her voice low as she started to come out of her lethargy.

"I saw your face at the window and told Lucas Grant. He came back to look for you."

"What about the other girl?"

"Sarah?" Hannah's stomach tightened. "She's my sister."

"No, another girl. I never saw her, but they talked about her. Her name was Rosie."

"Rosie Glick?"

Belinda nodded. "They said they needed to find her."

"But...but I thought they had her."

"I can only tell you what I have heard." The girl rubbed her arms. "They mentioned a basement."

"The basement of the lodge?" Hannah asked.

"I am not certain."

Hannah stopped the car and turned to face Belinda. Even in the dark she could see her wide eyes and fearful expression.

"Have you ever driven a car, Belinda?"

The girl hesitated.

"I need to go back and tell Lucas about Rosie, but I can't leave you in the middle of the woods. So answer me truthfully—do you know how to drive a car?"

The girl dipped her head. "Do not tell my father, but I have driven with the man who promised me nice clothes and pretty jewelry."

How ironic that after everything that had happened, Belinda was worried about her father finding out she had driven a car.

"I won't tell your dad," Hannah assured her. "Continue on this path. It will intersect with the main road. Turn right and you'll end up at the inn. Alert the sheriff. He's in room three."

"But what about you?"

"I need to go back," Hannah insisted.

"They will capture you."

"I have to help Lucas."

She climbed from the vehicle and held the door for Belinda, who quickly settled in behind the wheel. "Don't turn on the headlights until you get to the main road. It's about five hundred yards from here."

The girl caught hold of Hannah's hand. "*Gott* protect you."

"And protect Lucas, Sarah and Rosie, as well."

She closed the door quietly and watched as Belinda drove away. Then, turning, Hannah ran back along the path she had just traveled. She had to get to Lucas. She had to get to Lucas in time.

"Hey, Josh, the boss wants to see you." A guy cupped his hands around his mouth and called from the doorway to the kitchen.

Lucas offered an internal prayer of thanks as the guard hesitated for a long moment and then double-timed it to the lodge. Once the kitchen door closed, Lucas shoved the guy with the limp toward the rear of the truck and opened the door.

"Climb in, buddy. We'll see how you like being tied up and defenseless."

The guy dug in his heels and shook his head. Lucas shoved him into the truck, bound and tied his hands and feet, and jammed a rag in his mouth. He tied the guy down so he couldn't roll and then quietly closed the door and hurried to the side of the cottage. Once again he peered into the bedroom window and saw the blonde woman sitting on the chair where Hannah had been earlier.

The delivery-truck driver wearing the Braves baseball hat and windbreaker came into the room, grunted and then left, leaving the door open. Lucas stretched to see into the main room, where a security guard stood, coffee cup in hand.

Two men. Could he take them?

Only if he could divide and conquer.

He rooted in the grass and found two small pebbles.

Glancing around the side of the cottage, he lobbed one of the small stones at the porch. Again, he peered into the window. The guard sipping coffee placed his cup on the mantel and headed for the door.

He stepped onto the porch, walked to the van and peered through the window. Lucas slammed the butt of his weapon against the guy's head. He collapsed without a sound.

With swift, sure moves, Lucas bound and gagged him and tucked him inside the truck along with the first guy. Only one man remained, but when Lucas stepped from the van his heart stopped.

The driver from Savannah—Mr. Baseball Cap and Windbreaker—was standing with his weapon raised. Only his weapon wasn't pointed at Lucas. It was pointed at the person held in a tight hold against his chest.

"Hannah!"

NINETEEN

"I'm sorry," Hannah moaned. "I wanted to help you, Lucas, but I've done everything wrong."

The guy glared at Lucas. "Drop your weapon."

"Don't hurt her." Lucas removed the gun from the holster around his waist and placed it on the ground.

"Hands over your head."

Lucas complied.

"Who's in the truck?" the guy demanded.

"No one of interest."

"That's not smart, Amish. Open the doors so I can see inside."

"You're from Savannah. I've seen a picture of you on Olivia Parker's phone. Remember her? You killed her on the dock. First you called her and told her a woman was being trafficked. Then you ambushed Olivia when she showed up."

The guy sneered. "I didn't know there were Amish folks in Savannah."

"You didn't think anyone saw you, but your picture has been sent to law enforcement in the city. They plan to apprehend you and Vipera."

"That's Mr. Vipera to you, but you're a fool if you think he can be taken down. Mr. Vipera is above the law."

"Tell me what he does with the women."

"If I tell you, I'll have to kill you."

Lucas smiled. "You plan to kill me anyway."

"What about her?" the guy asked, jamming his gun against Hannah's chest.

"She doesn't deserve to die."

"Of course not. She'll make a nice addition to Mr. Vipera's entourage. The Amish ladies are always so agreeable."

"Where's he keep them?"

"You've heard of his island? He entertains wealthy businessmen from counties around the world. The ladies are one of the extra benefits he provides."

"Is that what happens at the lodge?"

"On a much smaller scale. The pleasure industry is lucrative and Mr. Vipera pays well."

"Is that why when a woman escaped some weeks ago everyone was upset? Someone started stalking the woman's sister. He said he wanted information, but he really wanted a substitute for the woman who escaped."

"You're talking about Tucker Davis. He had

an agreement with Mr. Vipera. Once an agreement is made, the contract needs to be fulfilled. Mr. Vipera doesn't want anyone to cheat him out of something he's purchased."

"Women aren't chattel."

"Some are." The guy laughed.

Lucas stared at Hannah, his mouth dry, his heart racing. He needed to throw the gunman off with a series of false claims. Hopefully when frustrated, the guy would make a mistake.

"Two men are dead," Lucas taunted. "But they told me everything about the operation before they died."

"They didn't know anything," the guy countered.

"I called the Savannah-Chatham Metropolitan Police Department and talked to the chief. He'll make sure Vipera is arrested."

"Amish don't have phones."

"But I'm not Amish. I'm an undercover cop. What will happen to you when the chief tells Mr. Vipera that you're the snitch?"

"What?"

"I told him you blamed Olivia's death on Mr. Vipera. I said you provided evidence."

Lord, let him buy into this story I've created, Lucas prayed.

"I sent the chief photos of her dead body and said I got them from your phone," he continued.

"Anything is possible these days with a good computer and a little technical expertise. I also created photos that showed Mr. Vipera at the crime scene. How long will it take his henchmen to find you once they learn you provided evidence that could send Mr. Vipera to jail?"

"Oh, Lucas," Hannah gasped.

"Shut up." The guy tightened his hold.

"No." She struggled, kicked his shin and bit into the flesh on his arm.

The guy growled and shoved her aside.

He aimed his weapon at Lucas. Hannah threw herself against the gunman and knocked him off balance.

Lucas charged. He ignored his aching leg and ran headlong into the guy, dropping him to the ground. His weapon flew into the brush.

Lucas pummeled his chest, then landed a blow to his chin.

The guy groaned and passed out.

Lucas started to get up and saw Hannah, gun in hand.

"I would have killed him to save you." Her voice was hollow and devoid of inflection. "Maybe I understand what you were feeling with Olivia."

"You thought I wanted to kill him, but I just wanted to bring him to justice."

"What about the men in the van?"

"They're both very much alive." He glanced over his shoulder. "We need to get going before the guards come back. While I tie this guy up, you go inside and free the other woman."

"Is it Sarah?"

"Hannah, I don't think—"

He wanted to warn her but she was already gone.

Hannah raced into the cottage, hurried to the bedroom and pushed on the door. "Sarah," she cried, opening her arms.

Then she stopped short.

The blonde woman was her sister's age but she wasn't Sarah.

TWENTY

Sirens sounded when Hannah stepped onto the porch with the young woman. Three police cars pulled up to the rear of the lodge, lights flashing. Two cars from the Willkommen sheriff's office and two more from the Petersville police department parked at the front entrance.

One officer in a squad car stopped at the cottage. "You folks get in. I'll take you someplace safe. We're not sure how everything will go down."

"A number of security guards are inside the lodge," Lucas said as he helped the women into the car. "Three guys are in the back of the delivery van."

The cop relayed the information over his radio.

"How did you know we needed help?" Lucas asked.

"Ned Quigley's the acting sheriff in Willkommen. He just got back from GBI headquarters in

Atlanta and pulled us together. The guy's good. He knows law enforcement."

It was over, almost over. Lucas put his arm around Hannah. She folded into his embrace and cried all the way back to the inn.

Hannah wouldn't let Lucas out of her sight. Too much had happened too fast. The sheriff and Fannie sat in chairs by the fireplace while Lucas stood next to where she sat on the couch. The hot coffee Fannie had made helped to steady Hannah's trembling heart.

Deputy Gainz had driven the two women home. Belinda had been reunited with her family and promised to never be so foolish as to believe an *Englisch* man who promised her pretty things. She wanted to talk to the bishop, to be baptized and to live within the Amish faith.

Hannah looked up at Lucas, seeing the fatigue on his face, but she also saw the sense of purpose in his eyes. She had been wrong. He wasn't focused on the past. He was thinking of the future. He touched her shoulder and she raised her hand to his.

The sheriff put down the cell phone. "They didn't find Rosie. In fact, everything in the lodge seemed legit. Evidently the trafficking was done in the cottage at the rear of the property. The Savannah police are on their way to

Vipera's home to arrest him. The coast guard is headed to his island. Federal agents are on board."

"I hope they find the women and reunite them with their families." Fannie glanced at Hannah. "I am praying Sarah will be among those found."

That was Hannah's prayer, as well.

"Vipera will get the best lawyers," Samuel continued, "but they're confident the men Lucas hog-tied will talk. Seems that story you made up, Lucas, about being undercover and sending photos you claimed came from their phones to incriminate Vipera did the trick. Plus, the women who have been held captive will be credible witnesses. I have a feeling there will be an abundance of evidence to bring Vipera to justice."

The sheriff smiled with appreciation. "The chief of police in Savannah said to thank you, Lucas. He also said if you wanted your old job back—"

Lucas held up his hand. "No way. I'm staying in Willkommen."

"Ned Quigley's running things until I get back on my feet, but I could still use another deputy," the sheriff offered.

"And take the inn's new manager away from me?" Fannie said with a huff.

She smiled at Lucas. "I'm getting older. Having Hannah with me made me realize how much I missed spending time in my own home. I'm ready to turn over more of the inn's operation to a competent manager, if that's the type of job you're interested in having, Lucas."

He beamed with gratitude. "That sounds perfect, Fannie."

"I guess we just need to know what Hannah plans to do." Fannie smiled. "I need someone to help me in the office, if you're interested in a permanent job."

Everyone looked at her. She could feel the heat rise in her cheeks. "I…I don't want to go back to Macon, and I don't want to go back to the way I was living. If you need me here, Fannie, I'd like to stay and work at the inn."

"I need you, of course, but I think someone else does, as well." Fannie winked at Lucas and then patted the sheriff's arm. "Might be good to stretch your legs, Samuel. Your physical therapist said you need exercise."

He took the hint and the two of them left the room.

Lucas pulled Hannah to her feet and smiled down at her, causing her heart to beat wildly. Without saying a word, he drew her closer. Then he lowered his lips to hers. She molded against him, overcome with a sense of acceptance and joy.

"Everyone seems aware of the way I feel," he said when their lips finally parted.

"Everyone except me," she answered coyly.

"I've fallen in love with you, Hannah Miller."

"Oh, Lucas. I love you, too. You're a good man and I'm sorry that I thought you harbored vengeance in your heart. Evidently I couldn't see clearly enough because of my own struggle. I told you that I learned about my father the night I left my mother and sisters, but I never told you what else I learned. He was a thief and also a murderer. He gunned down three people in a church and killed two police officers as he was fleeing. All this time, I've feared law enforcement mainly because I thought they would look unfavorably on me because of the sins of my father."

Lucas started to speak but she touched her finger to his lips, needing to explain everything she had been holding back. "For the last three years, I harbored resentment toward both my mother and father. Seeing how you brought Olivia's murderers to justice made me realize that I needed to forgive my parents so I could move on with my life."

"Your father has no bearing on who you are, Hannah."

She nodded. "I know that now. I've forgiven him and forgiven my mother, thanks to you."

He rubbed his hands down her arms. "You're beautiful, Hannah, and sensitive and smart, and you make life worth living again. It's soon, I know, but I want you to hear what my heart is saying…"

Her own heart was ready to explode. She stepped even closer.

"My heart says it loves only you. Will you be my wife? Will you let me love you and cherish you for the rest of my life?"

"Oh, Lucas, I love you, and, yes, I want to be your wife. Nothing would make me happier."

"There's one condition, as you probably know."

She tilted her head, suddenly worried about what he expected, what caveat he would place on their love.

"I want to become true Amish, to be baptized into the faith and to live my life within the Amish community. It's not an easy choice, and I know you probably need more time."

Relief flooded over her. "When I thought you would return to law enforcement, I knew I wouldn't be able to follow you back to Savannah. What I've found here, in this peace-loving community with their focus on the Lord, is what I want for my life, too."

"I need to talk to the bishop. Hopefully he'll realize I no longer harbor vengeance in my heart or desire retribution. I'm free of the past and ready to embrace the future."

Again, Lucas lowered his lips to hers and pulled her more tightly into his embrace.

Eventually he eased up a bit and smiled. "We'll have children together."

She nodded. "A houseful."

"I'll work the land and manage the inn."

"I'll learn how to cook on a woodstove and how to bake bread and delicious pies."

"And we'll face tomorrow together."

"Nothing could be better." She pulled him closer and turned her mouth to his. "Now, my sweet husband-to-be, stop talking and kiss me again."

"*Yah*, kissing is a good thing. *Ich liebe dich*, Hannah Miller. I love you."

She wrapped her arms around his neck and whispered before his lips touched hers. "*Ich liebe dich*, Lucas Grant. I love you now and will love you forever. Cross my heart."

EPILOGUE

Hannah stood next to Lucas and peered over the clearing, seeing the green grass and the budding trees in the distance. Turning, she spied the deer stand where everything had started on that fateful night.

So many things had changed since then. Instead of her earlier apprehension toward law enforcement, she now felt only gratitude for Ned Quigley, Deputy Gainz and especially dear Samuel. She glanced at where he and Fannie stood, hand in hand, both somber and lost in thought.

With Lucas's help, the three men from the Willkommen sheriff's office had brought down a state-wide trafficking operation. Tucker Davis, the guy in flannel who had come after her, was in jail awaiting trial, along with a handful of other men who had been involved in the mountain operation. The men Lucas had subdued at the lodge had copped a plea, and because of the information they had provided, the Savannah district attorney felt confident Eugene Vipera would pay for his crimes.

Lucas slipped his arm around her shoulders. "Are you okay?"

She smiled, appreciating his concern. Glancing down at the freshly covered grave, she was overwhelmed with a sense of closure. Her mother had been laid to rest in this idyllic setting, on Lucas's land, almost at the exact spot where he had saved Hannah for the first of many times.

"I was just thinking about everything that happened and how God protected both of us." She hesitated, feeling the weight of concern she carried in her heart. "If only—"

He pulled her close. "They'll find Sarah. God will hear our prayers."

She nodded, appreciating how her soon-to-be husband always said what she needed to hear. "I'm praying for Rosie Glick, as well."

"'Patience is a virtue' is what the bishop told us before we were baptized."

She rubbed his arm and smiled. "My mother claimed I was impatient to a fault. I understand her better now. She struggled to accept God's love and, evidently, never felt loved herself. I hate that she had to carry such a cross. Hopefully the Lord healed that brokenness before her death."

"What about the letter? Have you opened it yet?"

She nodded. "My father hopes I'll keep writing. He said he never knew what happened to me. My mother left him when I was six months old, but he's kept a picture of me all these years."

"If you decide to visit him in prison, I can—"

Hannah shook her head and held up her hand. "Not yet, Lucas. I'm not ready. Maybe someday."

"We have time, Hannah. A whole lifetime ahead of us."

She kissed his cheek, thankful for his strength and understanding. Taking his hand in hers, she stepped back from the graveside and together they walked to where Fannie and Samuel stood.

"Thank you for being here," Hannah told them both.

"Of course, child. You're like family." Fannie opened her arms and Hannah stepped into her warm embrace, feeling a connection and a love that she had always longed to receive from her own mother.

"You'll need a marker for the grave," Samuel said, ever the pragmatist. "Something simple with her name."

Hannah appreciated his suggestion and smiled,

knowing how the kindly man seemed a perfect match for Fannie. Perhaps soon he would be ready to embrace the faith of his youth.

No doubt aware of his fatigue, Fannie patted Samuel's hand. "Let's go back to the inn. Lunch will soon be served and I know you are hungry."

As they turned to retrace their steps, Hannah stopped short, seeing the handsome Amish couple who had climbed from their buggy at the far side of the clearing.

"Looks like we've got company," Samuel announced.

Tears welled up in Hannah's eyes and her heart nearly burst with joy. "Miriam," she called as she ran with outstretched arms to her sister, her beautiful sister who had come back to Willkommen.

"Hannah." Miriam's long skirt billowed out behind her as she raced across the clearing, wisps of hair pulling free from her bonnet.

A flood of tears spilled down their cheeks as the two women embraced. "My sweet sister, I have missed you so." Miriam's words were like a balm that healed Hannah's long-ago broken heart. In that split second everything was forgiven and the wounds of the past were forgotten. Now only this present moment mattered.

An Amish man, tall with broad shoulders,

shook Lucas's hand, and then the two men embraced, as well.

Fannie and Samuel joined in the welcome.

Miriam and Hannah didn't need words. They would catch up later. Now they just basked in the knowledge that yesterday had passed and they were together again.

Arm in arm, they walked to their mother's graveside, both women silent, each lost in her own thoughts.

"I'm sorry I left you," Hannah whispered at last, the words and the memories no longer painful.

"I still don't know what happened that night," Miriam admitted. "Later, Mother told me how much she loved you and missed you. She regretted her actions, but she could never muster the courage to call you. I regret not doing so. Maybe I wanted to punish her for forcing you to leave."

"She's at peace now," Hannah said.

Wiping their tear-streaked cheeks, the sisters walked to where the men they loved waited.

"I'm hungry," Samuel grumbled.

"I'd like to invite all of you to the inn for lunch," Fannie announced, taking Samuel's hand. "I hope you'll join us there."

Eager for the welcoming comfort of the inn, the two other couples climbed into their buggies. Hannah hesitated and glanced back over the clearing, overwhelmed with gratitude for the many ways the Lord had blessed her life.

Lucas kissed her cheek and then stared down at her with eyes of love. "As Fannie would say, *Gott* is good."

Overcome with emotion at the bounty of the Lord's providence, Hannah wrapped her arms around his neck and smiled at the wonderful man who had stolen her heart. "Sarah will come home soon. I know it, Lucas, especially now with Miriam here. Today we will celebrate as a family."

"We need to tell them about our upcoming wedding."

She nodded. "We have to tell them about a lot of things, but first, I need to tell you something, Lucas Grant."

He took off his hat and pulled her closer, his eyes twinkling. "*Yah*, I am waiting to hear what you will say, my little cabbage."

She laughed then feigned a pout. "But I wanted to be your brussels sprout."

"Ah, *liebling*, you are my everything."

They laughed, and when the laughter stopped she said what she had wanted to say and would continue to say for the rest of their lives. "I love you, Lucas."

He lowered his lips to hers and all she had ever wanted was fulfilled in his kiss.

"Let's go home," he said, helping her into the buggy.

Snuggled next to him as Daisy started down the path that led back to the inn, Hannah's heart nearly burst with joy. *Gott* had given her what she had always wanted, a man to love and a place to call home.

* * * * *

If you enjoyed UNDERCOVER AMISH,
look for the first book in the
AMISH PROTECTORS *series,*
AMISH REFUGE.

Dear Reader,

I hope you enjoyed *Undercover Amish*, Book 2 in my Amish Protectors series that follows Book 1, *Amish Refuge*. Attempting to find her missing sisters places Hannah Miller in the middle of a human-trafficking ring, and the only one who can help her is Lucas Grant. The former cop left the Savannah police department eleven months ago. Since then he's been working for a kindly Amish innkeeper and is ready to join the Amish faith, but when Hannah's life is in danger, he knows Hannah is more important than his future. The problem is Hannah can't trust anyone involved in law enforcement, especially a handsome guy who harbors a dark secret that could threaten not only her safety but also her heart.

I would love to hear from you. Email me at debby@debbygiusti.com or write me c/o Love Inspired, 195 Broadway, 24th Floor, New York, NY 10007. Visit me at www.DebbyGiusti.com and at www.facebook.com/debby.giusti.9.

As always, I thank God for bringing us together through this story.

Wishing you abundant blessings,
Debby

Get 2 Free Books,
Plus 2 Free Gifts—
just for trying the Reader Service!

Get 2 Free Books,

Plus 2 Free Gifts—

just for trying the Reader Service!

YES! Please send me 2 FREE Harlequin® Heartwarming™ Larger-Print novels and my 2 FREE mystery gifts (gifts worth about $10 retail). After receiving them, if I don't wish to receive any more books, I can return the shipping statement marked "cancel." If I don't cancel, I will receive 4 brand-new larger-print novels every month and be billed just $5.49 per book in the U.S. or $6.24 per book in Canada. That's a savings of at least 19% off the cover price. It's quite a bargain! Shipping and handling is just 50¢ per book in the U.S. and 75¢ per book in Canada.* I understand that accepting the 2 free books and gifts places me under no obligation to buy anything. I can always return a shipment and cancel at any time. The free books and gifts are mine to keep no matter what I decide.

161/361 IDN GLWT

Name _____ (PLEASE PRINT) _____

Address _____ Apt. # _____

City _____ State/Prov. _____ Zip/Postal Code _____

Signature (if under 18, a parent or guardian must sign)

Mail to the **Reader Service:**
IN U.S.A.: P.O. Box 1341, Buffalo, NY 14240-8531
IN CANADA: P.O. Box 603, Fort Erie, Ontario L2A 5X3

Want to try two free books from another line?
Call 1-800-873-8635 today or visit www.ReaderService.com.

* Terms and prices subject to change without notice. Prices do not include applicable taxes. Sales tax applicable in N.Y. Canadian residents will be charged applicable taxes. Offer not valid in Quebec. This offer is limited to one order per household. Books received may not be as shown. Not valid for current subscribers to Harlequin Heartwarming Larger-Print books. All orders subject to approval. Credit or debit balances in a customer's account(s) may be offset by any other outstanding balance owed by or to the customer. Please allow 4 to 6 weeks for delivery. Offer available while quantities last.

Your Privacy—The Reader Service is committed to protecting your privacy. Our Privacy Policy is available online at www.ReaderService.com or upon request from the Reader Service.

We make a portion of our mailing list available to reputable third parties that offer products we believe may interest you. If you prefer that we not exchange your name with third parties, or if you wish to clarify or modify your communication preferences, please visit us at www.ReaderService.com/consumerschoice or write to us at Reader Service Preference Service, P.O. Box 9062, Buffalo, NY 14240-9062. Include your complete name and address.

HOMETOWN HEARTS ♥

YES! Please send me **The Hometown Hearts Collection** in Larger Print. This collection begins with 3 FREE books and 2 FREE gifts in the first shipment. Along with my 3 free books, I'll also get the next 4 books from the Hometown Hearts Collection, in LARGER PRINT, which I may either return and owe nothing, or keep for the low price of $4.99 U.S./ $5.89 CDN each plus $2.99 for shipping and handling per shipment*. If I decide to continue, about once a month for 8 months I will get 6 or 7 more books, but will only need to pay for 4. That means 2 or 3 books in every shipment will be FREE! If I decide to keep the entire collection, I'll have paid for only 32 books because 19 books are FREE! I understand that accepting the 3 free books and gifts places me under no obligation to buy anything. I can always return a shipment and cancel at any time. My free books and gifts are mine to keep no matter what I decide.

262 HCN 3432 462 HCN 3432

Name	(PLEASE PRINT)	
Address		Apt. #
City	State/Prov.	Zip/Postal Code

Signature (if under 18, a parent or guardian must sign)

Mail to the **Reader Service:**

IN U.S.A.: P.O. Box 1867, Buffalo, NY. 14240-1867
IN CANADA: P.O. Box 609, Fort Erie, Ontario L2A 5X3

* Terms and prices subject to change without notice. Prices do not include applicable taxes. Sales tax applicable in NY. Canadian residents will be charged applicable taxes. This offer is limited to one order per household. All orders subject to approval. Credit or debit balances in a customer's account(s) may be offset by any other outstanding balance owed by or to the customer. Please allow 4 to 6 weeks for delivery. Offer available while quantities last. Offer not available to Quebec residents.